It wasn't so much the blood on the floor that Becky minded, as the way it kept coming back...

MISS ABIGAIL'S ROOM

CATHERINE CAVENDISH

Dedication

To Colin, without whom…

Acknowledgments

A massive 'thank you' to Crossroad Press
for being an amazing publisher

Chapter One

It wasn't so much the blood on the floor that Becky minded, as the way it kept coming back.

That morning, as she did with monotonous regularity, she heaved her bucket up the steep, winding stone stairs to the turret room, muttering to herself. She panted as she stood at the top of the stairs and stared at the heavy oak door. A warm August sun streamed in through the turret windows in the east tower of the large eighteenth century country manor. Sweat beaded Becky's brow, and she wiped her hand across her forehead, catching up a stray lock of mousy brown hair which she tucked, none too successfully, under her white housemaid's cap.

Her heart beating a little too quickly, she took a deep breath and reached for the door handle, praying that, just once, she wouldn't have to get down on her knees and scrub away the gruesome stain.

She turned the handle and pushed the door open, peering into the still, darkened bedroom. "'Ere goes."

The room smelled of emptiness. Miss Abigail had been away for three months this time, but she would be back in a week or so. At least that was what the butler, Mr. Farnsworth, had told them all at breakfast.

Heaving another sigh, she tugged at the dark green damask curtains that hung on one wall of the semi-circular room and sunlight flooded in. Despite the summer warmth, Becky shivered. She hated this room. Its heavy atmosphere always left her depressed and gloomy.

Her view was uninterrupted for miles across Stonefleet Hall's immaculate, velvet green lawns, over the trees to the rolling Wiltshire hills beyond. The bright sun against the deep azure sky made her squint, and she wished she didn't have to turn around. But it had to be done.

"Oh Gawd! Not again."

There on the floor to the left of the window, the familiar splash of red stained the parquet floor.

Hitching up her black skirt, she groaned as she lowered herself onto her knees, wincing at the pain of her Housemaid's Knee. "I'm getting too bleedin' old for this lark."

Taking her rag, she sloshed it in the galvanized bucket, wringing it out before plopping it onto the floor and setting to her task.

Ten minutes later, she tossed the rag back into her bucket and sat back on her haunches, mopping sweat from her forehead with a grimy handkerchief. "Stay away this time, why can'tcha?" Becky's joints creaked as she heaved herself upright, almost tripping as her boot caught on the hem of her skirt, ripping it. "Dammit! Now I'll 'ave to get me needle and thread to it again. Gawd knows 'ow much more mending it can take."

A sudden noise caught her attention. She gazed around the room, taking in the tidy double bed with its heavy white cotton bedspread, the wardrobe with its doors shut tight, and the mantelpiece covered in delicate china ornaments.

Becky hardly dared breathe. All she could hear was her own heartbeat. Yet, she was sure she had heard something, a slight knocking sound when there should be nothing. No one else had any reason to be up here. The only room in this turret was Miss Abigail's, and the only person in that room was Becky.

And she wasn't staying any longer than she had to.

In an instant, she opened the small transom window sufficient to let in some fresh air, grabbed her rag and bucket, and left the room, shutting the door firmly behind her. Then she was across the tiny landing and down the steps as fast as her aching legs and sloshing bucket would allow.

At the bottom, she paused to catch her breath before returning to the basement servants' hall — the closest thing to a real home Becky had ever known. Just walking in there slowed her heartbeat and put the world back where it should be.

The room was below ground level and sunlight struggled to penetrate the small windows. It had a homely feel about it. Comforting aromas of roasting meats and baking wafted through from Mrs. Beddows' adjoining kitchen.

The butler was sorting through the mail. He looked up as she entered, peering over his wire-rimmed spectacles. "Have you cleaned Miss Abigail's room?"

Becky lowered her bucket to the stone floor. "Yes, Mr. Farnsworth, and that stain was back again. I knew it would be. Like I said to Sarah, there's something not right in there." She sat on a high- backed wooden chair at the table where the servants took their meals.

"Don't be silly. It's a fault in the wood. I understand they have a similar problem at the Palace of Holyroodhouse in Edinburgh. The maids have been dreaming up all sorts of fanciful notions about its origins."

"But Mr. Farnsworth, it ain't right in that room. It's awful."

"Becky! Don't let me have to reprimand you again. I have spoken to you before about those terrible 'penny dreadfuls' you've been reading. Now, have you done the grates in their lord and ladyship's rooms?"

Becky sighed and picked up her bucket. "Yes, Mr. Farnsworth. I done them before I did Miss Abigail's room." She made her way toward the scullery to empty her bucket.

"I trust you didn't disturb her ladyship. She needs her rest."

"No, Mr. Farnsworth. She slept peacefully all the way through." As she would most of the day, thought Becky, judging by the almost empty bottle of laudanum she'd seen on her night table.

Becky returned from the scullery, putting her cap straight and smoothing down her apron. Despite the summer day, the dark room was cool, and Becky was grateful for the small fire that burned in the grate.

Lily—the new kitchen maid—had the hard work of cleaning out the ash and setting and lighting the fire every morning before the other servants were up and about. Her efforts meant that not only were the servants kept warm, but a ready supply of hot flat irons was always available when needed.

The other servants were elsewhere in the house attending to their chores, their routines unchanging from day to day. Sarah, the head house parlor maid, would be cleaning the drawing room while Sam Jenkins, his lordship's valet, would be assisting his master in dressing for the day. The cook—Mrs. Beddows—and Lily would be busy preparing breakfast for upstairs, although with only his lordship around to eat it, they wouldn't be too stretched.

"The 'ouse is ever so quiet, isn't it Mr. Farnsworth?" Becky said, cupping her hands around the teapot on the table. Finding it still quite warm, she smiled and fetched herself a cup and saucer from the sideboard. She didn't mind stewed tea. Most of the time, that was what she ended up with anyway.

The mail sorted and placed on a small silver tray, Mr. Farnsworth removed his glasses and sat at the head of the table, declining Becky's proffered cup of tea with a dismissive wave of his hand.

"I suppose we must all get used to a quieter life. Miss Abigail spends so much of her time up in Lancashire at the cotton mill, and her ladyship's health is indifferent since...the accident."

Becky paused in mid-sip and put her cup down onto her saucer. "Yes, about that accident. I mean, it was six years ago and I've never really understood what went on. I know it was up at the Burnley mill and there was workers killed, but I never really got to the bottom of it."

The butler stood abruptly. "That's quite enough gossiping for one morning. You can help Sam when he gets back from attending to Lord Stonefleet. All the silver needs polishing for Miss Abigail's homecoming. And there's no call for that expression!"

Becky hated polishing the silver. She hated the smell of the polish and the way her hands were black afterward. Nevertheless, she knew better than to defy Mr. Farnsworth, so she trudged off to the butler's pantry to collect the best cutlery and begin the task.

Sam joined her a half hour later.

"What a life, eh?" she said as the two of them scrubbed away at the silver dessertspoons.

Sam raised his eyes to heaven. "By rights I shouldn't even be doing this. It's not my place. I'm his lordship's valet."

"Well, who else is there to 'elp me?" Becky stabbed at the pink silver polish with her cleaning rag. "His lordship's so measly, he's not replaced 'alf the servants. We're short at least two 'ousemaids, and that new girl Lily's 'aving to do the job of kitchen maid *and* scullery maid. It's not right, I tell you."

"You're not wrong there. I reckon we're all put upon far too much in this household. In my last place, the master's valet wouldn't have been seen dead doing some of the jobs they expect me to do here."

"Cyril will be the next to go, mark my words. Then they'll 'ave you driving his lordship's carriage and looking after the 'orses. See if they don't."

Sam snorted. "Over my dead body and that's a fact." He stopped polishing. "I'm concerned about his lordship though. His clothes are hanging off him, and he seems to have shrunk somehow. His trousers will all have to be taken up."

"He does look sickly, doesn't he?"

Sam nodded. "Lord Stonefleet was always a big man. And he was imposing, with that great booming voice of his. He always seemed angry about something."

"I know what you mean. He's hardly recognizable these days. I reckon he's sickening for something."

"He won't see Dr. Stamford. I know. I tried. Tore me off a right strip, he did."

Becky paused in her polishing and gazed off into the distance. "Something in this house is wrong, you know."

Sam nodded. "You're right there. It all started with that accident. It was a happy place to work until then. After that, her ladyship took to her bed and everything changed. Suddenly there were no parties, no weekends away. Nothing. Then she had that heart attack and now she just lies there."

"Poor soul. She takes far too much of that laudanum, if you ask me. Too much of that stuff sends you potty." Becky looked around her, making sure the butler wasn't in sight, but they were all alone in the servants' hall. "I was up in Miss Abigail's room this morning. And it was back again. That blood."

"Get away! Really?" Sam's eyes widened, and he leaned closer, his cleaning rag poised halfway between the polish and the tablespoon he was shining.

Becky nodded. "And I swear I 'eard a strange noise. Like someone knocking."

"What? Like someone was trying to get in?"

"I dunno. Maybe. But the door was open." She shuddered. "Something ain't right in that room. There's always this funny smell — like something old and dusty. Old paper, maybe. Or books. And Miss Abigail 'erself... Well, put it this way. She's never been the same since she came back from her uncle's plantation in America. When was it? Two years ago? Spends all her time up at the mill in Burnley. It don't seem right a lady like her working with all those rough men."

"Oh, I don't think she actually *works* with them. As far as I can make out from what his lordship's told me, she lives in the house up there and looks after things for him. Makes sure his manager runs things properly and doesn't swindle him out of the profits."

Becky leaned back and polished a couple more spoons in silence, her mind churning things over. Something had been bothering her for a long time, and she needed to see what Sam thought. "Have you noticed anything different about Miss Abigail recently?"

"I don't see much of her even when she's here so can't say I have, no. Why? What do you mean?"

Again Becky looked around. She leaned forward, as did Sam, and they met halfway across the servants' dining table. "She's got this sort of distant look in her eyes, and she never spends any time with her father. Sees her mother now and then but most of the time when she's 'ere, she's in that blessed room of 'ers, miles from anyone. What does she do up there all day? That's what I want to know."

She saw Sam's expression change and felt someone behind her. Mr. Farnsworth. And he was bristling.

"It is not for the two of you to speculate on Miss Abigail's comings and goings. Have you finished polishing the silver yet?"

"Not yet, Mr. Farnsworth," Sam said.

"Then I suggest you both work in silence to get the job done quicker. I don't want to hear another word from either of you until that silver is gleaming."

Becky opened her mouth to protest.

"Not another word. Don't forget that there are plenty of girls out there who would be only too willing to take your job if you don't want it. Remember that, my girl, although you shouldn't need to be reminded. Not with your background." Mr. Farnsworth could never resist an opportunity to remind her of her humble origins on the streets of Hoxton, a filthy, poverty-and-disease-ridden part of north London.

The butler turned on his heel, and Becky pulled a face at Sam, who smiled and lowered his head. The two of them knew better than to argue with the stern butler. Ever since the housekeeper had retired six months previously, he had assumed her role as well as his own. Even with the entire west wing of the large house empty and closed up, his responsibilities were onerous. Maybe too much so?

Mr. Farnsworth was even tetchier than usual, these days. She would have to watch herself; she couldn't risk being thrown out on the street without a reference. Everyone knew what happened to women in those circumstances and, even in her happiest moments, Becky knew her youth was behind her. At thirty-three, she was catching sight of the first gray hairs, and those joints of hers were not what they were even five years ago. All the years of kneeling on hard floors, scrubbing and polishing, had taken their toll. They had robbed her of all the childhood dreams that had let her mind travel far from the harsh reality of the squalid room where she had lived with her parents and five siblings.

She had dreamed of running free on sweet-smelling grass, like the immaculately tended lawns here at Stonefleet Hall, of being able to feel the sun on her face and the wind in her hair, her face flushed with health, not sallow with lack of sunlight. What she would give to have experienced that. She sighed and brushed away a tear. Life was cruel and unfair, and no mistake.

A rustle of starched apron and the sound of boots on flagstones were followed by their owner, Sarah, clearly not in the best of tempers. Becky lowered her polishing rag and waited for the inevitable tirade.

"I thought you'd cleaned that stain in Miss Abigail's room."

"I *did*."

"Well, you couldn't have done it very well, because I stepped in it!"

"That's not right. I scrubbed that floor clean, I did. But every time I do it, that bleedin' stain comes back." Becky shuddered. "It ain't natural, I'm telling you. There's something wrong in that room. Either that or someone's playing nasty tricks." She glared at Sam, whose jaw dropped.

"Don't look at me, Becks. I haven't even been in there. I'm not allowed in Miss Abigail's room. Her being a single lady and all."

The butler appeared at the door. "What's all this commotion?"

"Becky's been slacking again," Sarah said, "She didn't clean Miss Abigail's floor properly."

"Honestly, Mr. Farnsworth, there's something not right in that room. Not right and not Christian. There, I've said it."

The butler's mouth was set in a firm line. "Nonsense, Becky. Go back upstairs with your bucket and do that floor again."

Becky's eyes widened, and her stomach did a somersault. She couldn't face another encounter with that room. Not today. She would have to make an excuse. "Oh, Mr. Farnsworth, do I 'ave to? I'm that tired—"

"If you had done your work properly, you would have every right to be tired but, from what Sarah says, you clearly haven't. Don't let me have to repeat my orders."

All eyes were on Becky. She looked from one to the other and, as always, felt inferior. There was Mr. Farnsworth in his smart butler's uniform, Sarah with her perfectly starched white apron, her light brown hair swept up into a bun from which not a single hair dared to escape, and Sam in his smart black valet's suit. In contrast to them, Becky's hair eluded her creased white cap, her apron was stained with silver polish, and her boots needed a good shine. Not to mention her fingers, which were sore from the combined effects of an array of household chemicals and carbolic soap.

She knew when she was beaten. Hoisting herself up from the table, she trudged into the scullery, returning momentarily with a bucket of steaming hot water and a half smile on her face. She might be beaten, but she wasn't going without gaining one small victory. Not if she could help it.

"Can Sarah come with me, Mr. Farnsworth? Her eyes are younger than mine. Maybe she'll see if I miss a bit." She smiled at Sarah, who scowled at her. Becky knew only too well that the maid had been looking forward to an hour or so in the chair with a cup of tea and her feet up.

Mr. Farnsworth looked up at the large wall clock with its pendulum swinging back and forth, marking time and directing the order and routine of the entire house. Three o'clock.

"Very well, Sarah. Off you go, and make sure she does it properly this time. You can dust Miss Abigail's ornaments. Carefully, mind. We don't want any breakages."

Sarah glared at Becky, who continued to smile sweetly back at her.

"Yes, Mr. Farnsworth." Sarah half pushed Becky out of the servants' hall, closing the glass-paneled door behind her. "You knew I wanted a sit-down this afternoon."

"And you know I cleaned that floor proper this morning, but you 'ad to land me in it with Mr. Farnsworth, didn't you?"

"I don't know anything of the sort. For all I know, you did miss a bit. Leastways, that stain was there half an hour ago."

They had reached the bottom of the turret stairs, and Becky had one hand on the banister when a thought struck her. "What were you doing in Miss Abigail's room? You couldn't 'ave been dusting, because you're going to do that now."

Sarah looked flustered for a moment and then regained her composure. "None of your business." She gave Becky a push. "Get along with you."

As she made her laborious way up the staircase, Becky wondered what Sarah's reaction meant. What *had* she been doing in there? She shook her head and concentrated on ensuring she didn't trip.

"You'll have to repair that tear in your skirt when you've finished up there. I'm surprised Mr. Farnsworth didn't notice. You really should be more careful. His lordship isn't made of money, you know. He can't keep shelling out for new servants' uniforms all the time."

Becky muttered an oath under her breath.

They arrived at the top of the stairs, and Becky stared at the gnarled oak paneled door. "That room gives me the creeps, with or without that stain. I can't imagine why she likes it so much."

"You're too fanciful. Like Mr. Farnsworth says, Miss Abigail has had that room since she was a little girl. Ethel used to clean it, but she's gone to work for Lady Garston, so you have to do it. Come on. Sooner we start, the sooner we'll be finished, and we can have a nice cup of tea and you can mend that skirt."

Becky looked at her curiously. In less than a minute, Sarah had gone from scolding her to being almost friendly. Really, was anything going to make sense today?

She watched Sarah turn the handle. As the door opened, they stepped forward to enter the room.

Sarah gasped. Becky let out a shriek and almost dropped her bucket.

Every single ornament was smashed, and the blood was not only back but smeared over the walls and curtains.

Becky jerked backward, heedless of the sloshing water from her dropped bucket. Sarah slammed the door shut and the two women hugged each other, trembling with fear.

"My God, Becky, who—what—could have done that? Do you think an animal got in? Or a seagull?"

Becky's teeth were chattering so much she could hardly speak. "That weren't no animal, and it weren't no seagull neither."

A piercing scream rang out from downstairs. "Her ladyship!" Sarah hiked up her skirt and raced down the turret stairs. Becky followed, less swiftly. They met Mr. Farnsworth on the landing at the top of the main staircase.

"You go to her ladyship, Sarah. Becky, go back down into the servants' hall and wait with Mrs. Beddows in the kitchen."

"But—"

"*Now*, girl. Don't argue!"

The rotund, gray-haired Mrs. Beddows was wringing her hands and sobbing when Becky arrived.

"Oh, what's happening, Becky? Why did her ladyship scream? It was like a banshee. I wouldn't have thought she had it in her to make such a fearful noise. She's such a little bird these days. There's hardly anything of her."

Becky approached the chattering, middle-aged cook and took her hand. "Sarah's with 'er, Mrs. Beddows. And Mr. Farnsworth's there too—"

The sound of running footsteps coming closer stopped her in mid-sentence. Mr. Farnsworth appeared at the door.

"Becky, fetch Dr. Stamford. There isn't a minute to lose. Her ladyship's in a bad way."

This time Becky didn't need telling twice.

———

"It was awful." Sarah's hands shook as she recounted what had happened in her ladyship's room. All the servants were gathered around the dining table. Mr. Farnsworth sat at the head while Mrs. Beddows positioned herself opposite him at the far end. Sarah was directly opposite Becky, who was glued to her every move and word.

Sarah continued, "When I first got there after her ladyship screamed, I saw her in bed, and she seemed to have fainted. She was lying half in and half out. I tried to lift her, and she moaned a little and seemed to be trying to raise her head. Then she opened her eyes, but I couldn't tell if she could see me or not. They seemed sort of glazed over." She paused as if trying to collect her thoughts.

"Go on, Sarah," Mrs. Beddows said. "What happened then?"

Sarah ran her tongue over her thin lips and took a sip of tea before continuing. "Well, she said the oddest thing. I said, 'It's me, Sarah, my lady,' and she looked straight at me. This time, I knew she could see me. She said, 'It was here. Right here. In this very room.' So I said, 'What was here, my lady?' And then she said something I didn't understand."

"What was it?" the butler asked. "What did she say?"

"'Nemesis,' Mr. Farnsworth. She said something called Nemesis had come to take her away. And then she died, right there in my arms."

There was a gasp followed by a shocked silence from the servants. Only the sound of Sarah's heartrending sobs penetrated the dim basement room.

Chapter Two

"It's just a room, Becky. Go in there with your mop and bucket and clean it. Then put fresh linen on the bed."

"But what about the mess? The broken ornaments and all the blood everywhere?" Panic welled inside Becky. It would almost be better to run out of this house and never look back than have to face that awful room again. Almost. But not quite. She could never face going back to Hoxton. No matter how bad things got here.

Sarah tutted impatiently. "Look, Becky, I'm not telling you again. A bird got in that room and flew about. You yourself left the window open. It probably caught itself on something and that's why there's blood on the walls. You'll have to change the curtains too. Best use the ones we took down from the old nursery when we shut up the west wing last year. I'm sure they'll fit that window."

Becky hesitated, trying desperately to think of a valid reason why she should not have to face that awful room. Nothing came to her fast enough, and Sarah was becoming agitated.

"Go on. Go and clean that room, and I'll be up later to check you've done it properly. And no missing the corners. You know how particular Miss Abigail is. She'll be home tomorrow and in no mood for any nonsense. She'll be grieving for her poor mother and have a lot to organize with the funeral and all."

Becky heaved the big copper kettle off the kitchen range and stomped off to the scullery, where she found Lily washing dishes. Becky glanced at her while she poured hot water into her bucket.

Lily carried on washing the servants' lunch crockery in silence. She was a funny little thing. Hardly said a word and never went out anywhere on her days off. She just stayed in her little bedroom off the scullery. Goodness alone knew what she got up to in there all on her own. At least in the attic, Becky had Sarah for company. They had single iron beds in one small room with a plain wooden dressing table and mirror on which sat a large ewer and washing bowl, filled every night with cold water for their morning wash. Lily had a wooden bed but had to use the scullery sink to wash in.

Poor Lily. In days gone by, there would have been another maid to share the work, but hard-pressed though she was, she never complained. Two months she'd been there, and Becky didn't know any more about her now than she did on that first day when a shy knock at the kitchen door had revealed a slight, pretty girl of no more than sixteen. Her fair hair had been tightly wound into a bun, and she had the largest pair of vivid blue eyes Becky had ever seen. Lily only came up to her shoulder. Couldn't have been more than four feet ten, if that, and when she did speak, her voice was like a whisper that got lost on the breeze.

Becky sighed and added cold water from the tap to the steaming bucket. "Are you going to the funeral, Lily? I could lend you a hat if you haven't got one suitable."

Lily looked at her, smiled vaguely, and shook her head.

Becky tried again. "Bet this is a bit different to your last place, isn't it? Mind you, it didn't used to be like it is 'ere now. Back when I first started, right up until six years ago, this house used to be full of servants. There were always huge dinner parties and people coming to stay for weekends. Very important people used to sit at the big dining table upstairs.

We've even had royalty. The Duke of Clarence came 'ere. And government ministers. Once I can remember Mr. Disraeli complimented Mrs. Beddows on her saddle of lamb." Becky sighed and heaved her heavy bucket onto the floor. "Those were the days. Now you'd think his lordship hadn't two ha'pennies to rub together. 'Course, Mr. Farnsworth says—"

"And what does Mr. Farnsworth say?"

Becky spun on her heel and was confronted by the butler's grim expression.

"Nothing, Mr. Farnsworth. I was getting my bucket ready to go and clean Miss Abigail's room."

"Well, go to it, girl, and less gossiping. You're distracting Lily from her work and not getting your own done."

"Yes, Mr. Farnsworth. Sorry, Mr. Farnsworth."

Bucket in one hand, she grabbed the nursery curtains from where she had put them on the dining table and scurried off as fast as she could.

At the top of the turret stairs, Becky faced the door. She licked her dry lips and pushed the inevitable stray lock of hair back under her cap. Under one arm, she had tucked the nursery curtains, and she had set the bucket on the floor beside her.

"It's only a room. That's all it is. A bird got in and hurt itself. It got scared. It fluttered around and its wings broke all the ornaments." She repeated the same words to herself as she put out her hand and gingerly turned the handle.

The door always needed some encouragement, and no amount of oiling its hinges could stifle the groaning noise they made every time they were required to perform their task. Today was no exception, and Becky held her breath, fearful of what might lie on the other side.

She paused for a moment or two before putting a toe over the threshold. Then she peered around the door, ready to run at any second.

Apart from the usual odd smell of old parchment and its oppressive atmosphere, everything was as it had been last time. The room was in a mess, but at least there was nothing else to add to the disarray.

Becky glanced at the floor. The stain was back. "Like a bad penny."

Reaching behind her, she picked up the bucket and entered the room, leaving the door wide open in case she felt the need to make a swift exit.

"Might as well start with you," she addressed the stain, then heaved herself down on her knees, her floor-cloth in hand. A slight breeze ruffled the blood-spattered curtains. Finally satisfied she had removed all traces of the stain, Becky hoisted herself up, leaning on the broad window-sill for support. She looked up and saw the small transom window was still open a few meager inches.

"Must have been a pretty small bird." She glanced around the room at the mess of broken porcelain strewn all over the floor and bed and the spatters of blood on the white walls. "It certainly did a proper job while it was 'ere though. Wonder what 'appened to it."

Becky shuddered. She hated finding dead things. Sometimes she would find a shriveled mouse in the larder and it always gave her the willies. It dragged up childhood memories of mummified rats and putrefying cockroaches in the filthy hallways of that tenement in Hoxton.

She peered around the room, expecting at any moment to see a forlorn little corpse of a wren or, at most, a sparrow. But there was nothing. It must have escaped.

She climbed on a nearby chair and unhooked the soiled curtains, praying the new ones would be long enough. Fortunately they were, and Becky stood back to admire her handiwork.

For a moment, she wondered if Miss Abigail would notice. But she knew Miss Abigail didn't miss much and would most certainly note the presence of a pair of curtains she had grown up with at her nanny's side.

Becky started on the walls, relieved to find that the blood came off quite easily. She was careful to use the tip of her forefinger wrapped in a clean, white cloth, and she prayed the water wasn't dirty enough to leave a smudge. But for once, she was in luck.

Next, Becky picked up a wastebasket from beside the dressing table and began to fill it with shards of porcelain. Shame about all those broken keepsakes.

His lordship had given his daughter most if not all of them over the years. Mementos of his many trips abroad.

As she filled the bin, Becky wondered how Lord Stonefleet must be feeling with his wife gone and him all alone in that great big house. He had been out, touring the grounds with his estate manager, when Lady Stonefleet had died so suddenly. Becky hadn't seen him since and Mr. Farnsworth was tightlipped when she tried to wheedle any information out of him, saying only, "His lordship is naturally upset but is, in accordance with his station in life, maintaining a dignified calm."

Dignified calm indeed! Why didn't he bawl his eyes out like normal people? Sam didn't seem to know anything either. He had told her that his lordship hardly said a word to him, and his eyes had a constant faraway look. Not that Sam saw much of him anyway—only when his lordship needed to be washed and dressed or retire for the night. The rest of the time, whenever he rang the bell, Mr. Farnsworth went up to him.

"As long as I live, I'll never understand the upper class. Oh Gawd, there I go again, talking to meself. I swear, they'll send the men from Bedlam to come and take me one of these days!" Becky chuckled as she threw the last of the broken ornaments into the bin.

She picked up the final object and stared at it. Nasty. "Urgh!" She threw the thing away from her and it landed on the bed. It seemed to be some sort of doll, only about four inches long and fashioned out of wax. A candle, maybe, but deliberately shaped into a figure that looked male. Overlapping, downy black feathers were stuck to it to form a suit, and a nose, eyes, and mouth had been crudely drawn on, perhaps with charcoal. But the thing that made Becky recoil for the second time was not the doll itself, but rather the darning needle that had been thrust into its chest area.

Nausea billowed up inside her, and she felt hot and sweaty. The room became oppressive. She wiped her dripping forehead as the adrenalin swirled.

She had to get out of that room. As fast as she could, she grabbed the dirty curtains and wastebasket with one hand and the bucket with the other. She had just made it to the doorway when she heard a deep, heartfelt, male sigh. And she knew, without looking, the sigh had come from that doll.

Panting hard, Becky hurried down the stairs as fast as her skirt and burdens would allow her.

Becky blinked in the darkness and pulled her sheet closer around her neck. "It ain't right."

"What isn't?" Sarah said from across their bedroom.

"Making a doll like that and sticking needles in it. Why would anyone make such a thing? It's not like it's a pretty toy for a child to play with."

She heard a deep sigh from her fellow maid. "I wouldn't know, Becky. I haven't seen it."

"Go in tomorrow, before Miss Abigail gets back. I threw it onto the bed and it should still be there. You'd better be careful though."

"Why?"

"I swear it sighed. It made this sort of moaning sound. Like someone in pain." Despite the humid warmth of a sultry August night, Becky shivered.

Sarah laughed. "Oh, Becky, that imagination of yours. It'll get you into such trouble one of these days. You see if it won't. Now get to sleep. We've got to be up at five thirty."

She heard the sheets rustle as Sarah made herself comfortable for the night. Soon the sounds of gentle snoring would start.

Becky's mind wandered to Miss Abigail's room. She pictured the wax doll, lying on that bed. What was it doing? Was it sighing? Or maybe moving?

She pulled the sheet over her head.

———

"Well, I've been up there and there's no doll in that room, so that's an end to it. You must have dreamed it. I told you that imagination of yours would get you into trouble. Let's not hear anymore about it."

They were alone in the servants' hall. Becky paused in the act of mending a frayed cushion cover and stared at Sarah in disbelief. "Someone must 'ave moved it after I left. They must 'ave gone into that room and took it away."

The maid laughed and carried on pressing her apron with a flat iron. "Oh, yes, I expect Mr. Farnsworth decided to play a practical joke on you and went in there when you weren't looking. Oh, come on, Becky. You made a mistake. Forget about it and get on with your work. You've still got the grate to do in the morning room, and Miss Abigail will be here in a couple of hours."

"Yes, indeed, Becky. You should listen to Sarah." The butler had appeared at the door, his pocket watch in his hand. "Get along with you, and don't forget to put on a clean apron and tidy yourself up as soon as you have finished. I want all the servants in the hall ready for Miss Abigail's homecoming."

"Is his lordship going to be here to greet her?" Sarah asked.

"His lordship is feeling…indisposed and will be remaining in his room this morning. I must go to the wine cellar. We will be needing a bottle of the Margaux as it's Miss Abigail's favorite. The 1870, I think. It was an excellent vintage, and I'm sure his lordship would approve."

Becky watched the butler retreat. "Anyone would think his lordship was avoiding his own daughter." She fingered the cloth she would use to polish the morning room grate.

"They used to be so close. Before the accident."

"Yes. Strange 'ow everything changed then, isn't it?"

Sarah put down the iron. "What do you mean?"

"Well, her ladyship used to be so busy with her committees and parties and all. His lordship was always off to the 'ouse of Lords or fox hunting or shooting. And all those country 'ouse weekends. I mean, this place was always filled to bursting with guests and dinner parties. Mrs. Beddows used to 'ave three kitchen maids at one time just to keep up."

Sarah sighed. "Yes, well, those days are gone, more's the pity."

Becky frowned. "It's like it stopped all at once. The accident changed everything overnight."

"It was a terrible tragedy. So many men, women, and children killed."

"Oh, I know, and I'm not saying any different. But I can never understand why her ladyship changed so much."

"She and his lordship were up there in Burnley when it happened. She must have been affected by all the sorrow and grief she saw."

"I suppose." Becky caught sight of the clock. "Oh Gawd! Best be off or I'll 'ave Mr. Farnsworth after me again."

"Yes, and you mind you're tidied up ready for eleven o'clock in the hall."

In the morning room, Becky laid down a white cloth across the carpet immediately in front of the brass grate and knelt on it, using a dustpan and brush to clean away the soot and ash that still managed to accumulate even when there was no fire. She carefully emptied the contents of her pan onto newspaper and folded it over, ensuring there were no gaps. Spilling ash onto this carpet would earn her a severe reprimand, not to mention the chore of having to clean it off. Next she got her cloth, dipped it in the brass polish, and carefully cleaned around the grate, taking pride in the way it gleamed.

She knelt back on her heels before hoisting herself up. Two ornate brass candlesticks stood either side of the mantelpiece, and Becky inspected them. A little bit of burnishing wouldn't go amiss on them either.

As she worked, she allowed her gaze to wander across the room to the large dark brown leather Chesterfield settee, the writing desk by the window, and the glass display cabinet with its contents of Bohemian and Austrian crystal. A couple of comfortable yet elegant chairs completed the picture.

Her eye caught something that shouldn't be there. She stared in disbelief.

Becky replaced the candlestick on the mantelpiece and hurried over to the small ebony table that was the source of her consternation.

"It can't be 'ere. 'Ow can it be 'ere?"

There on the table, the wax doll leaned against a Tiffany lamp, this time, minus the darning needle.

"Becky, get a move on, will you?" Sarah gave her a push through the door leading from the servants' hall. "And get that hair tucked under your cap. Mr. Farnsworth will have something to say else."

"But you've got to believe me. It was there. Bold as brass. Sitting on the table. I swear it was grinning at me. That thing's alive, I'm telling you. It's alive and it's evil. That's what it is."

"Oh, get away with you. Stand next to Lily and pay attention to Mr. Farnsworth."

Becky's mind registered a protest, but her mouth wisely refused to utter it.

Outside, they could hear horses' hooves coming up the wide gravel drive. They stopped. One of the horses whinnied.

The butler straightened his tie. "Now, everyone. Quiet, please. Miss Abigail has returned." He smoothed his jacket and opened the front door.

A familiar, aristocratic female voice rang out. "Good morning, Farnsworth."

"Good morning, Miss Abigail. Welcome home. The staff and I are only sorry it had to be under such sad circumstances."

"Thank you."

Miss Abigail came into Becky's view. Her tall, slender figure was draped in black crepe and lace, with matching jet earrings and a necklace. As always, Becky was mesmerized by her face. It reminded her of a porcelain doll in Miss Abigail's own nursery.

Under her large black hat, her gleaming raven hair, showing a little gray at her temples, had been elegantly coiffured by her personal maid, Violet, who appeared, carrying a small bag. Becky watched Miss Abigail's charcoal eyes scan their way along the line of servants, briefly alighting on Becky. As they did so, the maid felt the intensity of her gaze and had to look down at her shoes, wishing she had given them a polish.

"Is my father at home?" Miss Abigail's voice was, as always, clipped and lacking any warmth.

"Yes, Miss, but I'm afraid his lordship isn't feeling very well this morning. He is in his room and hopes to join you later this evening for dinner," the butler said.

"Thank you, Farnsworth. I am rather tired after my journey. The overnight accommodation was not all that it could have been, so I think I will retire to my room."

"Very good, Miss."

Becky watched her almost glide up the stairs, followed by the thin and quiet Violet at her heels like a well-behaved lapdog.

There had been no word of concern from Miss Abigail about her father and, apart from her mourning dress, nothing to indicate she had lost her mother in sudden and unexpected circumstances. Nothing much of anything. Of course, she could just be tired, as she claimed, but...

Becky shook her head and followed the other servants back down the stairs to the servants' hall, all the while thinking and wondering. Sure something was very wrong indeed. At this moment, she wished with all her heart she could pack her bags and leave there.

But Becky had nowhere to go.

Chapter Three

"It don't seem the same without her ladyship." Becky blew her nose loudly while Sarah wrinkled hers at the sound. "I mean, she always seemed to 'ave something 'eavy weighing on her mind. Well, at least since the accident. And that 'eart attack she 'ad. Gawd knows, the poor woman knew suffering, but I'll miss 'er. It's like a piece of the 'ouse is gone."

Sarah nodded from across the table as she worked on her mending. "Do you suppose Miss Abigail will stay here, Mr. Farnsworth? Or will she go back up to Burnley after the funeral?"

"I am quite sure Miss Abigail will tell us of her plans when she's good and ready. Put that mending down, and Becky can lay the table for our tea." The cook appeared at that moment. "I am sure we are all looking forward to a slice of Mrs. Beddows' excellent fruit cake." He smiled at her and the cook preened.

The slight figure of Violet trotted in, neat in her navy blue skirt and white blouse. Becky noticed she seemed paler than usual and was frowning. "Miss Abigail is dining in this evening and says she will take tea in the morning room at half past four."

"Thank you, Violet," Mr. Farnsworth said.

Becky paused in the action of laying out knives and plates. "How's Miss Abigail taking the loss of her mother, Vi?"

Violet shrugged, but still the frown remained. "All right, I think. She doesn't talk about it much. Not to me anyway. When the news came to us, she was very quiet. Like she wasn't really taking it in and since then, she's just carried on."

Becky stared at her, perplexed. "You mean you ain't never seen her cry or nothing?"

Mr. Farnsworth's expression clouded. "I am quite sure that Miss Abigail feels the loss of her mother very deeply, but being part of the aristocracy, she doesn't go around weeping and wailing like a common fishwife."

"No, Mr. Farnsworth." Becky lowered her eyes.

But she still wondered.

"Is his lordship dining tonight, or is he still in his room?" Mrs. Beddows asked.

"I understand that his lordship will be dining with Miss Abigail," the butler said.

"Oh, good. I've got a nice bit of sole. I thought I'd do my *filets de sole Veronique*. It's one of Miss Abigail's favorites, and his lordship has always complimented me on it too."

"An excellent choice, Mrs. Beddows. I'm sure it will be much appreciated."

"It'll make a nice change to cook for upstairs again. I hope they make a habit of it. I am that bored with making soup and scrambled eggs on a tray, I can tell you."

"Now, Mrs. Beddows, you know your soups are delicious and were a great comfort to her ladyship."

At the mention of Lady Stonefleet's name, Mrs. Beddows reached in her apron pocket for her handkerchief and dabbed her eyes. "Poor lady."

The servants were seating themselves at the table when Becky's attention was drawn to Violet, who was clutching at her side. "Here, Vi, are you all right?"

All eyes turned to the lady's maid, whose face had turned white.

"I don't know, I don't feel at all well." She staggered and slipped to the floor in a dead faint.

"Oh my lord!" Mrs. Beddows struggled to kneel beside her and the other servants rushed to Violet's aid.

"Don't crowd her, give her some air," Mr. Farnsworth pushed Sam and Sarah aside and felt Violet's forehead. "She's burning up. Quick, Sam, fetch Dr. Stamford. Sarah, you and Lily get her up to her bed and mind you don't disturb his lordship. I'll go up and see Miss Abigail."

Sarah stopped at the door. She turned, and Becky glimpsed an odd expression on her face. "But Mr. Farnsworth, Miss Abigail's in her bedroom. Shouldn't *I* go up to her?"

The butler hesitated for a moment. "Yes, very well. Off you go."

Sarah scurried away.

There was a slight moan from Violet, and her eyelids flickered. Mrs. Beddows held her hand. "She's that clammy, Mr. Farnsworth."

"Come on, Becky, I'll assist you. She'll have to be carried. I doubt she can walk by herself. Lily, you stay with Mrs. Beddows and put on hot water. The doctor may need it for Violet."

Between them, Becky and the butler half dragged the semiconscious maid up the four flights of stairs to her attic room. Becky was heaving and puffing when they finally arrived and laid their charge down on her bed.

"You undress Violet and put her to bed while I go downstairs and wait for Dr. Stamford."

"Right, Mr. Farnsworth."

As gently as she could, Becky unbuttoned Violet's blouse and eased it off her thin shoulders. Violet moaned again as she was moved.

"I'm sorry, Vi, but I 'ave to do it. You'll be more comfortable when you're tucked up in bed."

Becky slid off the girl's skirt and unbuttoned her boots before removing her long black woolen stockings. Still Violet moaned and tossed her head from side to side, her forehead, face, and neck glistening with sweat.

"I never knew someone come down with a fever so sudden in all my days," Becky said. "I mean an hour or two, maybe less, but a couple of minutes? And no sign of anything before then."

Violet stopped moaning, and her eyes shot open.

Bloodshot. Wild. She grabbed Becky's arm and squeezed it so tightly, the maid flinched.

"Whatever is it, Vi? What's the matter?"

Violet shot upright. "It's coming, Becky. I know it. You must get away."

"What do you mean? What's coming?"

"Nemesis, Becky. Nemesis." She fell back, unconscious.

Becky felt for her pulse, trying first one wrist and then the other. Nothing.

Violet was dead.

———

"I can't believe it, Mr. Farnsworth." Becky clutched her handkerchief as she sat at the table, surrounded by the other servants. Shock registered on all their faces, even the butler's. "I mean, one minute she was chatting to us all down 'ere and the next, she's took ill and, not 'alf an hour later, she's dead. I mean, 'ow is that possible? 'Ow?"

The butler shook his head and removed his glasses. "Dr. Stamford said it could be down to a number of things. Possibly acute appendicitis. That can strike very quickly. Violet may have been in some pain or discomfort for a while and chose to be stoical about it, hoping it would pass. Then, at just that moment, her appendix may have burst. We won't know until they have performed a post mortem."

Becky blew her nose. Something was troubling her. "Mr. Farnsworth, I know Dr. Stamford said she was delirious with fever before she died, but she said something about Nemesis. Just like her ladyship. What is Nemesis? I ain't never 'eard of it before and now I've 'eard it mentioned twice in one week. And in this 'ouse too."

All eyes turned to the butler, who polished his glasses with his handkerchief before replying. "I believe Nemesis is a classical reference. According to ancient Greek legend, she was the goddess of retribution who would ensure that evil deeds did not go unpunished and that anyone possessing undeserved wealth should not live to enjoy its rewards."

"But why would Violet talk about it? I mean I never saw her reading no Greek stories."

The butler shifted in his seat. "I have no idea, Becky. She was out of her mind with fever, after all."

"All the same. What did she mean?"

The butler replaced the glasses on his nose as all the servants continued to stare at him, waiting for an answer. "I am sure the answer to that lies between Violet and her maker. Let's have no more conjecture on the subject."

"But Mr. Farnsworth—"

"That's enough, Becky."

———

"Sarah," Becky said as the two maids were dusting in the drawing room the following morning. "What did Miss Abigail say when you told her about Violet?"

Sarah carried on dusting shelves with her feather duster as she replied. "Nothing much. It was all a bit strange, actually."

Becky paused in her task of polishing the marble grate. "What was?"

Sarah seemed to consider whether to say anything further. She glanced at the closed door before she spoke in little more than a whisper. "When I got to her room, I was about to knock on the door when I heard this scraping noise."

"Scraping?"

"Yes, like… Oh, I don't know. Claws or something."

"*Claws?*"

"It doesn't make sense, does it? I thought I'd imagined it, so I knocked anyway and listened with my ear pressed firmly up to the door and I heard strange sounds. Couldn't make them out, but it was like Miss Abigail had someone in with her."

"Go on with you!"

"Then Miss Abigail called, 'Come in,' so in I went." She paused.

"What 'appened next? Was there someone in there?"

"She was all alone, and her room was tidy. She was holding something in her hand."

"What was it?"

Sarah shook her head. "I'm not sure. It may have been a candle or something."

"Did it 'ave feathers on it?"

"I couldn't tell. It was very small, and she was clasping it so there wasn't much to see."

"So what 'appened next?"

"I told her about Violet and that we'd sent for Dr. Stamford, and she thanked me. Told me to go back to the others and that she would be down directly."

"And that was it? That couldn't 'ave taken long."

"No, only a few minutes. Then I came straight back downstairs."

"No, you didn't." Becky registered the surprise on Sarah's face when she said that. "You were gone at least 'alf an hour, and Miss Abigail didn't come down until just after you. Dr. Stamford 'ad to wait for her in the morning room. And that was after he'd done the necessary with Violet. Didn't you think it was a bit odd that in the short time you were up with Miss Abigail, the doctor 'ad been and Violet 'ad died, all in the space of a few minutes?"

Sarah's bemused expression worried Becky. It seemed her friend didn't understand what she was hearing.

Without another word, Sarah went back to dusting the shelves. Becky polished her grate, her mind in several places at once.

A few minutes later, Sarah spoke as if nothing had happened. "You finish in here and go and do the study. I'm off up to Miss Abigail's room. I'm going to be looking after her."

Becky looked up and over at the maid's straight back. "Oh, lady's maid now, are we? There'll be no living with you soon."

"Be quiet and get on with your work," Sarah turned on her heel and left the room.

"That girl's the devil of a long time up there," Mrs. Beddows said as she presided over the teapot the following afternoon. Mr. Farnsworth, Sam, Lily, Cyril Johnson the groom, and Becky sat around the table, waiting to tuck into Mrs. Beddows' justly famous plum cake. "Becky, you go and see what's happened to her. She went up to Miss Abigail's room twenty minutes ago, and we're waiting to have our tea."

"Yes, Mrs. Beddows." Becky pushed her chair back and stood, wincing as her right knee troubled her.

"You want to get some Elliman's Embrocation on that, Becky." Johnson laughed. "Does wonder for my horses' stiff joints. I'll rub it in for you if you like."

"*Cyril!*" Mr. Farnsworth said.

Cyril winked at Becky, who gave him a half-grin. She liked him. It wasn't often any half decent-looking man flirted with her, and even though there was nothing in it, she felt a thrill from pretending she was young and pretty. What she wouldn't give...

She left the servants' hall and started up the back staircase.

No sign of Sarah. As she approached Miss Abigail's closed door, Becky could feel that familiar growing sense of panic rising inside her. What if that stain was back? Or the awful doll?

She reached the top of the turret stairs, just the short landing away from that room. In front of her stood the oak door. The hairs prickled on the back of her neck, and she could feel goose bumps on her arms even in the warmth of the summer afternoon, with the sun streaming in through the window.

She stood right by the door and raised her hand to knock. She froze. A sound—like claws scraping across the floor. Exactly as Sarah had described.

Becky tasted blood from her bitten lip. She wanted to get back down those stairs as fast as her legs would carry her but knew if she went back, with no news of Sarah, she would be at the mercy of Mr. Farnsworth's angry tongue, not to mention Mrs. Beddows' fury at being kept waiting for her tea.

Taking a deep breath, she raised her hand again and then leaped back as she saw the handle turn.

The door opened.

Sarah. She smiled at Becky, her face otherwise expressionless. "Miss Abigail's gone out." She closed the door behind her and started down the stairs.

"Who was that in there with you?"

Sarah stared at her, and Becky was struck by the blankness of her expression. "No one. There was no one else there. Miss Abigail asked me to tidy her room for her, that's all." She started down the staircase.

Becky, knowing she was being lied to but not understanding why, followed close behind her. At the foot of the stairs she confronted her. "What were you really doing in there?"

Sarah's smile seemed pasted on her face, and her eyes did not focus on Becky's but on a spot somewhere above her head. "I told you. I was tidying for Miss Abigail. And you'll be pleased to know the stain has not returned. Everything's in order. We can join the others."

"Oh, there you are, Sarah." Mrs. Beddows raised the teapot, ready to pour. "Come and sit down and we can have our tea at last."

Sarah did as she was bid, while Becky also sat, never taking her eyes off the maid.

Tea progressed as usual, and Becky watched in mounting amazement at the way everyone seemed to accept that the woman sitting drinking tea was the same one who had left them half an hour ago to go and see Miss Abigail.

Granted, she *looked* like Sarah. She *sounded* like Sarah. But why couldn't anyone see what was so plain to Becky? Whoever that woman was, sitting in the housemaid's place at the table, definitely *wasn't* Sarah.

Becky woke with a start.

A silver beam of light from the full moon scythed its way across the attic bedroom, illuminating the bed at the far end of the room near the door. Trying not to make a sound and disturb Sarah, she eased herself up onto her elbow and peered over.

Sarah's bed was empty.

Becky's gaze traveled over to the door. A dark shape—her dressing gown—hung on its hook, while next to it, where Sarah's should have hung, was an empty space. Maids were not supposed to go wandering around the house at night. But maybe Sarah couldn't sleep. Maybe she had gone downstairs to make herself some warm milk or cocoa. Or to the lavatory.

Becky had no idea of the time, but it had to be very early. Next to her stood a candle and some matches. She struck a match and lit the candle, its weak flame sending flickering shadows leaping across the whitewashed walls.

Becky pulled back the sheet and shivered as her bare feet touched the cold wooden floor. She stood and, taking her candle with her, went over to the mantelpiece to peer at the ancient, battered little clock. Ten minutes past three. She yawned and padded over to the door, opening it slowly to prevent it squeaking. The silent corridor was dark. No sign of anyone. Slowly, she closed the door and took her candle back to the night table.

Where had Sarah gone? She would wait up for her and find out. But Becky was simply too exhausted from her day's work to keep her eyes open for long and, within the hour, she had drifted back to sleep.

"Where were you last night, Sarah?" Becky looked carefully at the maid, who was sorting Miss Abigail's silk stockings.

"In bed. Same as you."

"No, you weren't. Leastways not at ten past three."

Sarah glared at Becky for an instant before the new bland expression that had drained all the character out of Sarah's face resumed its control. "I remember now," she said. "I came downstairs for a glass of milk. I couldn't sleep. Too hot."

"Oh, I thought it was quite chilly myself."

Sarah ignored her and carried on checking the fine stockings for snags or runs.

Becky polished a silver cream jug until she could see her face in it. She scowled at her reflection.

Wrinkles at the corners of her eyes and her mouth. Unmistakable. She was getting old. Miss Abigail was getting old too. There were wrinkles around her eyes as well. Becky had never understood why Miss Abigail had never married. She was eligible enough and there had been no shortage of suitors. Sarah had said no one could match her father, while Mrs. Beddows had speculated that maybe Miss Abigail was a little too intelligent and opinionated. "She scares them off," she had said when the last one departed to join his regiment in India.

Since the accident, Miss Abigail had rarely bothered. The flow of eligible young men had slowed to a trickle and, after she returned from learning about cotton on her uncle's plantation in Louisiana, there had been no one else.

There was no doubt in Becky's mind that the Miss Abigail who had returned from America was not the same woman who had gone there. Something had happened out there, and no one could have been more aware of it than her father, to whom she was barely civil.

Becky would have loved to know what had made her change so.

Sarah had changed too, and her ladyship and Violet had died so suddenly. What was happening in this house? Would she be next?

Sarah's sharp voice interrupted her dark thoughts. "When you've finished that, you can go and tidy his lordship's study. He'll be wanting to go in there at eleven, so look sharp."

Becky didn't answer. Instead, she folded the cleaning cloths away and tidied up. Taking her duster, she went up the back stairs, through the door into the entrance hall, and across the black-and-white tiled floor to the study.

The room smelled of leather and rich cigar smoke—comforting smells, warm and inviting. She tidied up yesterday's discarded newspapers, emptied and polished the ashtrays, and was dusting the table by a large winged armchair when the door opened.

Becky looked up and instantly dropped a brief curtsey. As always, when confronted with Lord Stonefleet, an army of butterflies shot into her stomach. His tendency to shout abuse at servants had come her way in the past, and she always felt she had to apologize for her presence. Head lowered, she mumbled, "Sorry, my lord, I was just finishing in 'ere."

But today was different. Lord Stonefleet seemed barely aware of her as he made his shambling way into the room. Becky tried hard to conceal her horror at his much deteriorated appearance. It had only been a few days since she had seen him and in that time his wife had died, but that didn't explain his stooped frame. He had always had a military bearing: tall and ramrod straight. Now, he favored his left side and rubbed his chest with his emaciated hand. His hair had become thin and was much whiter, leaving no memory of the fine head of black hair he had sported a mere two years earlier.

But the thin, reedy voice was the most shocking. "That's quite all right. You can go and fetch me a cup of coffee if you will."

Becky was taken even more by surprise. The politeness was almost more shocking than his appearance. "Yes, my lord."

"Has *The Times* arrived yet?"

"I think so, my lord."

"Very well, if you could bring that up, too."

"Yes, my lord."

Becky left the room as quickly as she dared and closed the door behind her, leaning against it briefly as she tried to make sense of what she had seen and heard.

Miss Abigail, dressed all in black, descended the stairs. "Ah, Becky," she said, her face hard. "Has my father come downstairs yet?"

"Yes, Miss Abigail. His lordship's in the study. I'm going to fetch him a cup of coffee. Can I get you one, too?"

"No, thank you."

She swept past the maid and opened the study door. Becky made her way quickly down to the kitchen, where Mrs. Beddows was rubbing fat into flour. Mr. Farnsworth was reading the newspaper.

"Here, Mrs. Beddows, I've just seen his lordship. Proper poorly he looked. And as for old... Well, he looked ninety if he was a day."

Mrs. Beddows picked up an egg, ready to crack and add it to the bowl. "Don't be ridiculous, Becky. His lordship's not a day over sixty-five. Is he, Mr. Farnsworth?"

"What's that?"

"His lordship. Becky says he looks ninety."

"Well, he does look ever so ill, Mr. Farnsworth.

Surely you must've noticed."

The butler's lips were set in a firm line. "His lordship is understandably grief-stricken at the sudden and tragic loss of his wife. I am quite sure he will be back to his old self in due course after the funeral. Now, have you done Miss Abigail's room yet?"

"No, Mr. Farnsworth. I thought Sarah was doing it."

"Sarah will be tending to Miss Abigail's needs as her lady's maid for the foreseeable future. Miss Abigail told me herself just this morning. As a result, you will need to assume her household duties."

Becky's temper flared to the surface, and her cheeks flushed crimson. "Oh, Mr. Farnsworth, that's not fair! I'm already doing enough for two maids and now Sarah's work as well—"

"*Becky!* That will be quite enough of that. Do I have to remind you yet again that the streets of Hoxton are full of young women who had the temerity to question the orders of their betters? Go up to Miss Abigail's room, make her bed, and tidy and dust everything so that it is spick-and-span. I have no doubt Sarah will inspect it later before Miss Abigail returns from Salisbury. That reminds me—Mrs. Beddows, Miss Abigail will be lunching out today, so there will just be his lordship. Miss Abigail felt a little consommé and a light salad would be appropriate."

Her presence no longer required, Becky scowled and stomped up the back stairs, her boots clattering on the stone. In the entrance hall, she met Sarah, dressed not in her parlor maid's uniform, but in a smart gray skirt and navy, high-necked blouse.

Again, Becky noted the blank expression in her eyes. "There'll be a vacancy," Becky said. "Now you're no longer 'ead 'ouse parlor maid."

"So there might be, Becky, but don't think it will automatically be yours. Not with your slovenly ways."

Despite the insult, Becky smiled. That at least sounded like the old Sarah. She watched her go through the door leading down to the servants' hall and kitchen, her back straight, not a hair out of place in the neat bun.

Becky trudged up the stairs, only remembering when she was halfway up the turret staircase that she had neglected to bring her bucket. "Oh Gawd, I 'ope it's not come back," she muttered.

She paused at the door, running her tongue over her suddenly dry lips. She leaned against it, listening hard for any sound.

Nothing.

She turned the handle and the hinges creaked as usual. But today they shouldn't have; Sam had only oiled them yesterday. She peered around the door.

Sun streamed in through the windows, and the curtains fluttered slightly in the light breeze wafting through the open transom window. "Let's 'ope we don't get any more birds in 'ere."

She looked at the floor. Clean. Mercifully, there was no trace of that awful stain. Maybe whatever caused it had dried up. Maybe Mr. Farnsworth was right and it had been something in the wood itself, like that other floor at that Scottish palace. Strange Ethel had never mentioned it, considering she had cleaned this room for years.

Becky shrugged and moved to the disheveled bed, where she began smoothing the sheets, fluffing the pillows and tucking in the blanket.

A noise behind her. She dropped the pillow on the bed and spun around. Something had moved. There. In the corner by the wardrobe.

She wanted to run, but this time, she was determined to conquer her fear. They'd only laugh at her downstairs and tell her she was imagining things again if she didn't.

She edged forward and bent down, until she could see into the small gap between the corner of the wardrobe and the adjacent wall. Something was there, all right. Something dark. A rat? A mouse? She recoiled but had to stare at it.

It didn't move. If she made a noise and the thing was alive, surely it would scurry away, and she could forget about it. At least for now. Becky clapped her hands. The thing stayed there.

Sweat breaking out on her forehead, Becky wrapped her hand in her duster and reached out. She screwed her face up and counted to three before grabbing the thing in the corner.

It felt small and solid. As she set it on the bed, at arm's length, she slowly unwrapped the duster and gasped.

The doll. This time its face was covered in red and yellow streaks, mingling with the black of its features.

Although there was no one there to hear her, Becky spoke out loud. Talking to herself helped calm her. "It looks like it's burning up. Them's flames. That's what they are. Mr. Farnsworth's got to see this. That'll stop them laughing at me."

Becky popped the pillow back in place and smoothed down the bedspread, carefully avoiding the doll. She retrieved her duster and carried on with her cleaning. She had to turn her back on the bed while she dusted the window frames and the sill.

Finished, she glanced back at the bed. "Where the bleedin' 'ell's it gone?"

She looked all around the bed, in it, under it, in the corner by the wardrobe. She searched every inch of that room, but the doll was nowhere to be found.

Perplexed, Becky sat in the chair by the window.

It didn't make any sense. That doll had been in the corner, and she had picked it up in her duster and put it on the bed.

"*Becky, Becky.*"

The voice was no more than a gentle whisper. The maid shot up straight.

"Who's there?"

Not Sarah, and definitely not Miss Abigail or Mrs. Beddows. The voice had been female, and a very light one at that. A thought struck her. Lily. But the kitchen maid had no business being upstairs. Besides, it might *sound* a bit like her but where was she?

Becky's mouth was so dry she couldn't even wet her lips. She placed her hands tightly on each arm of the chair and gently rose, for some reason fearful of making a sound.

"*Becky, Becky.*" This time, a light, tinkling laugh followed her name.

That was enough for Becky. Grabbing her duster, she shot out of the room.

Behind her, she could have sworn she heard that laughter again, but louder. Mocking her.

———

Lily was in the kitchen, drinking a cup of tea while Mrs. Beddows was busy in the kitchen. Becky's heart still pounded, but she wasn't going to risk any further ridicule by the servants so she decided not to mention what had happened in Miss Abigail's room. Besides, she hardly ever had an opportunity to get Lily on her own. The girl was so quiet she barely existed.

"Any more tea in that pot, Lily? I'm that parched."

Being the junior of the two, Lily was instantly on her feet. She selected a cup and saucer from the sideboard, and Becky watched her pour a cup of tea, which she handed to her. Becky added her own milk and two sugars and raised the cup to her lips, never taking her eyes off Lily, who sat back down, having not said a word. Her eyes were downcast.

"Are you settling in all right?"

"Yes, thank you." Her voice was faint, almost indistinct.

"You'll 'ave to learn to speak up a bit more 'ere."

Lily looked up, and Becky was taken aback at what she saw in the girl's eyes. Far from the demure little mouse, an icy fire blazed in those intense blue eyes.

"Yes. Thank you," she said, more loudly this time. And it sounded like a different person. One Becky wouldn't want to cross.

Goosebumps rose on her arms. "That's better," she said, hoping her voice didn't waver.

Lily looked back down at her cup again. The moment had passed.

An awkward silence followed. Mrs. Beddows called from the kitchen, "Lily, come and help me with this cheese sauce."

Lily leaped up from the table. "Yes, Mrs. Beddows."

Becky watched her race out of the servants' hall. "As if the devil was on her tail," she murmured, and shivered.

Chapter Four

Becky sat at the kitchen table, stoning raisins. "What do you know about that Lily, Mrs. Beddows?"

The cook paused in her task of folding flour into a mixture of egg and milk. "She's a hardworking girl, Becky. Gets on with her work and keeps her head down. You would do well to learn from her example, even if she is a good few years younger than you."

Becky chewed a raisin. "Where did she work before?"

Mrs. Beddows looked thoughtful for a moment. "I don't rightly remember. Miss Abigail engaged her up in Burnley, I think."

"She doesn't sound like she comes from up north."

"Well, you don't sound as if you come from 'round here either, with that London accent of yours."

"Maybe she moved there from somewhere then. Don't you find her awful quiet? I mean, she never speaks."

"I wouldn't say that. We often have nice little chats, her and me."

"What about?"

"I don't know. Something and nothing, probably. There now. I've forgotten to put in the sugar. I'll forget my own head next. You're distracting me, Becky, that's what it is. Have you finished stoning those raisins yet?"

"I'm on the last one." Becky slipped another one into her mouth.

"Yes, my girl. Well, if I had as many raisins for my cake as you have in your stomach, it would be a much larger cake. Get on with you!"

"Yes, Mrs. Beddows." Becky wiped her hands on her apron, ignoring the smear she left.

A bell rang.

"It's the front door. I'll get it." Becky limped up the stairs as fast as her throbbing knee would allow her. The pain was worse than usual today.

She opened the front door to Miss Abigail, whose expression was grim. Sarah followed her, carrying a hat box. Evidently Miss Abigail had been to her milliner.

"There is a dirty mark on your apron, Becky. Kindly change it immediately."

"Yes, Miss Abigail." Becky accepted the gloves, hat, and coat that were thrust out to her.

"Then you can bring me tea in the morning room. Is his lordship at home?"

"Yes, Miss. I believe 'e's in the study."

"Good. Kindly tell him I have returned."

"Yes, Miss Abigail." Becky had long since ceased wondering why father and daughter couldn't communicate their whereabouts to each other directly without the need for intermediaries.

Despite her previous encounter with a much subdued Lord Stonefleet, Becky felt her usual waves of trepidation, but she had her orders. There was nothing for it. She opened the study door and curtsied as she entered his lordship's presence. "My lord, Miss Abigail asked me to tell you that she 'as returned and is taking tea in the morning room."

Becky was surprised by Lord Stonefleet's reaction. He was sitting in a leather armchair reading his newspaper so she couldn't see his face as he was holding it up in front of him. She could, however, see how his hands shook, rustling the newspaper, at the mention of his daughter's name.

As if he was scared of her.

But why would Lord Stonefleet be scared of his own daughter?

Becky shut the study door quietly behind her and glanced up at the staircase. Things were certainly topsy-turvy in this house. Maybe it would all be better tomorrow, after the funeral. Becky offered a silent prayer before making her way up to her attic room to change her apron.

Sarah was there, packing a small suitcase. "Where are you going?" Becky asked.

Sarah didn't turn around, as she carried on folding her underclothes neatly and placing them in the case. "I'm moving into Violet's old room. Now I'm Miss Abigail's lady's maid, it is only fitting I should have my own room."

Becky shivered. "Violet died in that room only four days ago. I shouldn't like to sleep in a room where someone died."

Sarah closed her case. "Oh, I don't think I'll have anything to fear from Violet, Becky. Not where she's gone."

"Heaven, you mean."

"Not necessarily."

Becky stared at her. What a strange thing for a servant to say, especially one who had been brought up to attend church every Sunday and recite her prayers before bedtime.

Before Becky could ask her what she meant, Sarah had left her alone.

Tying on her clean apron, Becky checked her appearance in the mirror, tucking another stray lock of hair under her cap and straightening it. She spoke to her reflection. "That's something else that ain't right."

When Becky returned to the kitchen on her way to the servants' hall to start her mending, Lily and Sarah looked up at her. Lily was positioning a tea cloth onto a silver tray, and she and Sarah had clearly been in the midst of a conversation that ceased as soon as they became aware of Becky.

Lily and Sarah separated, but not before Becky caught a shared glance between them. In that moment, she had missed something important, something she needed to fathom out but which, for no reason she could rationalize, scared the wits out of her.

She went into the servants' hall and took out her workbasket from the tall cupboard in the corner. A lace doily she was mending lay over the top. She took it off and stared transfixed at the thing that lay underneath it. The grotesque doll's tiny black eyes seemed to fix her in its gaze, and she could swear its mouth was opening…

The box fell from her hands as she fainted, spilling its contents onto the floor.

———

"Becky! Becky!"

Mrs. Beddows' frightened voice was the first thing she heard. Becky's head buzzed as she struggled to sit up.

"Oh, thank the Lord for that. What on earth happened?"

Becky put her hand up to her throbbing temple and strained to focus on the circle of servants all peering anxiously down at her. As if through a fog, it started to come back to her. Her mending. The doll.

She looked around. There were the contents of her workbasket, strewn across the floor. "That doll. Where's that doll?"

Sam steadied her as she tried to stand upright. "What doll? What are you talking about?" Mrs. Beddows asked.

"That awful doll. The one I first saw in Miss Abigail's room. It was in my workbasket. That's why I fainted."

She saw Mrs. Beddows exchange worried glances with Mr. Farnsworth and, looking around at the other servants, fear started to rise in her.

"What's going on? Where's that doll? Did you find it?"

Mr. Farnsworth took charge, as always. "Now, Becky, you're clearly not very well, my girl. We've sent for Dr. Stamford and he'll be here directly. Come with Mrs. Beddows, and she'll see you get undressed and into bed. I'm sure everything will seem much clearer when you've had a good night's sleep."

"What? No, there's nothing wrong with me. I fainted, that's all. The shock of finding that bleedin' doll. I don't need no doctor."

But Mrs. Beddows ignored her protests as she, assisted by Lily and Sarah, half-dragged her up the stairs.

Becky pleaded with Sarah. "*You* know there's nothing wrong with me. I told you about that doll. I don't know 'ow it keeps turning up everywhere but someone's playing a trick on me. It's probably that Sam. Let me 'ave five minutes and a cup of tea and I'll be right as rain."

"No, Becky, you're not at all well, as you know. You told Lily and me you were feeling poorly yesterday, don't you remember?"

"What? I never…."

They were at the entrance to her bedroom, and Becky shrugged off the two maids, looking from one to the other of them. The mere sight of their glazed expressions sent shivers ripping through Becky's body. "Here, what's going on? What's the matter with you two?"

Mrs. Beddows opened the door. "Come along, Becky. Sarah and Lily will put you to bed."

Each maid took one of her arms, and Becky tried to fight them off. "I don't need to go to bed. And I don't want neither of you touching me. You're not right, you two. Something's got to you. Can't you see it, Mrs. Beddows?"

"Hush, Becky. Don't say such things or Dr. Stamford will have to send you away and you know what that means."

Terrible images flashed through Becky's mind.

Poor wild creatures in dirty shifts, screaming, yelling, tearing at their hair. Becky knew all about Bedlam and other places like it. If you went in there, you never came out, and if you weren't mad when they admitted you, the conditions meant you would be soon after.

Lily and Sarah had got her into her room and Mrs. Beddows was already half way out of the door, closing it behind her.

"Please don't leave me with them, Mrs. Beddows. *Please!*"

No reply. Becky struggled against the iron grips of both maids and wrenched herself free. "Leave me alone, you evil witches!"

Lily exchanged glances with Sarah and stood back against the door, barring Becky's escape.

"Now, Becky." Sarah's voice was soothing but it did nothing to allay Becky's fears. "Let's get you undressed and into bed before Dr. Stamford gets here. I expect you're overtired and maybe your blood's a little thin. You just need a tonic and a bit of rest."

Becky looked at her long and hard, knowing that she was outnumbered and, for now, would have to do as she was told. It didn't stop her from an urgent need to have her questions answered though.

"Who are you two anyway?"

Again, a shared glance between the two. A knowing look that did nothing to reassure Becky.

"Don't be silly, Becky. It's Lily and Sarah. Your friends."

Becky shook her head, her hair tumbling out of the makeshift bun. "You ain't Sarah, and you're certainly not my friends. I don't know who the 'ell you are, Lily. No one seems to know. Not even Mrs. Beddows. She can't even remember where you came from. Where was it again?"

Lily didn't answer. Her face retained its mask as she stood sentry, staring straight ahead of her. Not so much *at* Becky as *through* her.

Sarah took Becky's dress and handed her the clean, folded nightdress she had removed from the drawer of the wardrobe. "Put this on and let's get you into bed."

Becky said nothing. She did as she was bid, her eyes never leaving Lily's face.

When she was tucked in and propped against two pillows that Sarah had fluffed up for her, Becky addressed Lily. "You won't tell me where you came from or who you are but I know you don't belong here."

"That's not a nice thing to say," Sarah said, but the way she spoke just served to convince Becky that she was right in her suspicions. The old Sarah would have said the same thing but as a sharp reprimand, probably accompanied by a threat to report her to Mr. Farnsworth. This Sarah spoke the words, as if by rote, devoid of feeling.

Becky almost began a retort but thought better of it. What was the point? These two were not going to listen to her. From now on, she couldn't trust either of them. But who could she turn to? Not Mr. Farnsworth and almost certainly not Mrs. Beddows. Sam, maybe. Where was he today, anyway? Then Becky remembered he had gone into Salisbury on an errand for his lordship.

Lily opened the door and the two maids left, without another word. Becky heard the sound of the key turning in the lock. They weren't taking any chances on her escaping.

Her befuddled brain tried to make sense of what was going on. It all seemed to revolve around that doll and, as that had first appeared in Miss Abigail's room, it must be connected to her in some way.

Then the stain, which instead of mysteriously reappearing had stopped appearing at all. And what about the scratching noises she had heard from the room? The way Sarah had changed all of a sudden?

And poor Violet. How the girl had become ill and died within such a short time was incredible. It would be interesting to see what the post mortem revealed. Sarah had benefited from her death, too. All of a sudden, she had become a lady's maid.

An awful thought struck Becky. What if Violet's death had all been part of a plan? What if Sarah and Miss Abigail had plotted to murder Violet to make room for Sarah to step in? Becky could almost hear Mrs. Beddows' voice telling her not to be so fanciful.

But then, there was his lordship. For him to have aged and deteriorated as quickly as he had was unnatural, surely? Yet no one seemed to think anything untoward. Or if they did, they were very good at keeping it to themselves. Of course, Mrs. Beddows didn't see a great deal of him. In Miss Abigail's absence, he trusted her to run the kitchen, plan menus, order the food, and pay the tradesmen. All communication with her was through the butler, and Mr. Farnsworth was famously tightlipped about anything that was said or done upstairs.

All these thoughts tumbled through Becky's mind until she heard the sound of the key scraping in the lock. The door opened and the benevolent face of Dr. Stamford appeared.

"Now Becky, I hear you've not been eating properly."

She opened her mouth to protest but saw Sarah enter behind him and said nothing.

"You fainted in the servants' hall, I believe?"

"Yes, doctor, but it weren't 'cos I 'adn't eaten. It was 'cos I 'ad a bit of a shock."

Dr. Stamford extracted a stethoscope from his black medical bag, which he had placed on the night table. "Shock? And what was that, Becky?"

Becky cast a quick glance at Sarah who stood, expressionless, at the door. Damn her! She *would* say it. "It was a nasty doll thing, made out of a candle, I reckon. All twisted up and covered in black feathers. With a darning needle shoved through its 'eart. Leastways, it was like that the first time I saw it. Not this time though. And the first two times I saw it, it wasn't bent neither. First time, it 'ad the needle in its 'eart and the second time, the needle was gone but there was a blood stain. Well, it was *meant* to be a bloodstain. Don't know if it was real blood, of course. Then the next time—"

"Yes, yes, Becky." Dr. Stamford leaned her forward and pressed the stethoscope to her back. "Breathe in. Nice deep breath."

Becky did as she was told. He had barely heard a word she had said, no doubt dismissing it as a sick maid's ramblings.

"Very good. Your chest is clear."

"I never said it weren't."

"We have to eliminate all the possibilities. Let me take your pulse." He took Becky's left wrist. "It's a bit fast. Very fast, in fact."

"I'm not bleedin' surprised, doctor. You wouldn't believe what's been going on 'ere. It's enough to make anyone's pulse quicken!"

Dr. Stamford placed Becky's hand on the bedcovers and patted it. He turned to Sarah. "How long has she been like this? Excitable? Agitated?"

"A few days, doctor. Since her ladyship died." Becky stared at her, incredulously. "What?"

"Understandable, really," Dr Stamford said. "A loyal servant, distressed at her mistress's unexpected death. I'll prescribe a tonic. Plenty of rest and Mrs. Beddows' excellent food, and she'll soon be up and about again. But probably best if she doesn't attend her ladyship's funeral tomorrow. It could put her back."

Becky couldn't recall the last time she had felt so incensed. How *dare* they talk about her like this? "I am still 'ere and, despite what you say, I still 'ave all me wits about me."

Dr. Stamford turned back to her. "Yes, yes, of course, Becky. I quite understand."

"Begging your pardon, doctor, but I don't think you do."

"I can assure you, you're just a little run down. You need more iron in your blood, and the tonic I shall prescribe will be all you need to get you back on your feet."

"I wasn't off them."

Dr. Stamford gave her one final smile and handed the prescription to Sarah. "Have this made up straightaway. She should be up and about again in a couple of days."

"Thank you, doctor."

Becky heard the scrape of the key in the lock again, and she was alone with her thoughts. Far from feeling safe in her own little sanctuary, she had never been more scared in her life.

———

"Good to see you up and about again, Becky," Sam said as he pressed his lordship's suit.

It was late evening. Becky sat at the table in the servants' hall and picked up her mending. This time, she had to repair the ripped lacy trim on one of Miss Abigail's pillowcases. "I wasn't ill in the first place."

"No? Mrs. Beddows said that your blood was all thin and you needed a tonic and rest for a couple of days. Even missed her ladyship's funeral, and that was a grand affair, I can tell you. Everyone was there."

"Her ladyship was loved around 'ere, and rightly so. Poor lady. Never done nothing wrong and look 'ow she ended up."

Sam put the iron down and looked around before bending closer toward Becky over the ironing board. "To say she never did anything wrong is maybe pushing it a bit, Beck."

Becky's eyes opened wide, and she paused in her mending. "Oh? What do you know? Go on, tell me."

"Well, I heard it from Lord Stourton's valet. They've got that grand house up near Burnley."

"Yes, yes. Get to it."

"Well, about six years ago, her ladyship committed a little, shall we say, indiscretion."

Becky nearly dropped the pillowcase. "Her ladyship? With another man? *Never!*"

"Honest." Sam crossed his heart with his forefinger. "I was with him in the Dog and Duck last night. Lord and Lady Stourton came down for her ladyship's funeral and stopped for a few days with Lord and Lady Templeton-Hughes over at Templeton House. Edward — that's Lord Stourton's valet — wasn't used to cider. Said it was a sissy drink. So we plied him with a few pints." Sam laughed. "I don't think he thinks it's such a sissy drink anymore."

"Never mind that. What else did he say about her ladyship? Who was the man?"

"Well, that's the best bit. Apparently it wasn't a titled gentleman. In fact, it was no gentleman at all. According to Edward, Lady Stonefleet had it away with his lordship's foreman at the mill. Some poor bloke called Sidney Platt. Got himself killed in that accident."

Becky couldn't have been more shocked if Sam had told her he was running away to join the French Foreign Legion. "Get away with you. You're 'aving me on!"

"It's true. You ask any of them down the Dog and Duck. They'll tell you. He was well in his cups was Edward. Telling the whole pub about it, he was. Lord Stonefleet's bound to hear about it. And Miss Abigail."

"Make sure neither of them 'ears about it from you, that's all I can say. Messengers bringing bad news 'ave an awful 'abit of getting themselves shot."

Sam picked up the iron, touched its rapidly cooling surface with his finger, and took it back over to the fire, replacing it with one that was heated and ready. "Don't you worry, Becky, I'm saying nothing. Only to you, because I trust you."

"Thanks, I promise I won't say nothing." She thought for a moment. "Matter of fact, there's something I wanted to tell you. It's about..." Becky hesitated. Should she tell him? Could she trust him? But she had to tell someone, and Sam had always been friendly.

"Tell you what," he said as she pondered. "I'm about finished with his lordship's trousers. Why don't I make us a nice cup of cocoa and you can tell me all about it?"

"Ooh, yes, that'd be lovely."

Sam disappeared into the kitchen, and Becky finished her mending, put away her sewing basket, and carefully folded the fine pillowcase.

She was confident that Miss Abigail wouldn't be able to see the repair. Her tiny stitches had rendered it as good as new.

Sam returned and handed her a steaming mug of cocoa. "Go on," he said. "Spill the beans."

"All right. But you must promise not to say a word. Mr. Farnsworth will haul me over the coals again and Mrs. Beddows can't see nothing's wrong."

Sam moved closer to her, conspiratorially.

Becky licked dry lips. "It's Sarah. Well, Sarah *and* Lily, if you must know."

"What do you mean?"

"There's something very odd about Lily, and Sarah isn't... Well, 'aven't you noticed? She's not the *same*. Not since her ladyship died, and Miss Abigail got back. Not since Violet died. And I think that's got something to do with it."

"Eh?"

Becky's spirits plummeted. Sam was giving her that look of disbelief. Just like Mrs. Beddows and Dr. Stamford. She *had* to convince him.

"Look, I know this sounds odd, but I swear Sarah's changed these past few days. I can even tell you when it 'appened. It was a couple of days after Violet died, and she went up to Miss Abigail's room. She'd been gone ages and Mr. Farnsworth sent me to look for her. I went up and 'eard these scraping noises coming from inside."

"Scraping noises?"

Becky nodded. "Like claws scratching across the floor. I was about to knock when the door opened, and there was Sarah with the strangest expression on her face. Like her body was there but there was no one inside."

Sam shook his head. "I'm sorry, but you've got me there. I don't understand what you mean. Her body was there, but she wasn't? You hadn't been at Mrs. Beddows' cooking brandy, had you?" He laughed.

"No, I'm serious." She threw up her hands in frustration. "Why won't anyone believe me? Something 'appened to Sarah in Miss Abigail's room and she's not 'erself. It's as simple as that. Lily's the same. Only I didn't realize it at first, on account of she's new 'ere so I never knew her any different. But if you look at the two of them, their expressions are the same. They say the right words, but their eyes are dead."

Becky read the confusion in his eyes and wasn't surprised at his next words.

"If what you're saying is right, how did it happen? I mean, how did Sarah change? And why?"

Becky sighed. "I know it's 'ard to understand. I don't understand it meself, and I don't 'ave any answers neither. I wish I knew someone who did. I do think it must 'ave something to do with the dreadful doll that keeps turning up."

"Yes, what about that? I mean, by all accounts, you're the only one who's seen it."

Becky shook her head. "I don't know why that is and I don't know what it means, but I'm sure it's involved in some way."

Sam drained his cocoa mug and stood. "Well, all I can say is, it's a strange tale you have to tell and no mistake. I never heard anything like it."

Becky gave him a wry smile. "Neither 'ave I. But it gives me the creeps, I can tell you." She glanced up at the clock and yawned. Midnight. "Bed time."

"Night."

"Night, Sam."

Becky took the cups into the kitchen and poured a little water in each. Lily could wash them up in the morning with the breakfast things. She took one last look around the kitchen before turning off the gas lamps and mounting the stairs.

Tucked into bed, she lay on her back in the dark, thinking. The permanent feeling of fear throbbed in her head and echoed throughout her body.

Something evil had taken root here in this house. And it was coming closer.

"Becky. Becky."

She awoke with a start. Who was that? Someone had been calling her. She raised her head and listened. Still and quiet. The only sound was her heart pounding.

She lay back against the pillows. It must have been a dream. She closed her eyes.

"*Becky. Becky.*" The soft, female voice floated in through the door.

Becky leaped up and swung her legs to the floor. She grabbed her dressing gown from the back of the chair, wrapping it tightly around herself. She picked up the matches and lit the candle in its holder. Picking it up, she thrust her feet into her slippers and padded to the door, opening it silently. Outside, the corridor was dark, her candle making eerie, flickering shadows on the opposite wall. She stood for some seconds, listening. Nothing. Finally, she decided to go back inside.

"*Becky. Becky.*"

"Who's there?" She remembered to keep her voice down. She didn't want to wake Mrs. Beddows, although the cook was a sound sleeper whose hearing wasn't all that it had been.

A slight breeze ruffled the curtains at the far end of the corridor. The window was usually slightly open in summer, although Becky thought it had been closed earlier today. Maybe one of the other servants had decided to let in some air.

The breeze tickled her skin. "*Becky. Becky.*"

The voice was like a breath, transported on that breeze. Becky shivered and drew her dressing gown tighter around her. She wanted to dash back into her bedroom and shut the door tight behind her but something propelled her forward. Dream-like, she put one foot in front of the other and started down the corridor toward the fluttering curtain.

"*Becky. Becky.*"

The voice was still a breath, but closer. Becky limped down the stairs and along the landing leading to the turret staircase. With every footstep she wanted to turn and go back, but the faint voice kept moving her forward.

"*Becky.*"

She stood at the foot of the winding staircase leading to Miss Abigail's room. Her candle sputtered. What if it went out? She would be plunged into blackness.

Her mouth was dry, and she could smell that old papery aroma she always smelled in Miss Abigail's room.

To her relief, the candle held true, its flame settling to a gentle flicker.

Becky put one hesitant foot in front of the other up the stairs, gripping the banister with her free hand and taking care not to trip on her long nightgown.

She faced the door. Miss Abigail should be in there, fast asleep. There was no chink of light from under the door so she couldn't be reading.

Becky tried to swallow. It didn't help much. Fear had drained her mouth dry.

What now? She could hardly knock and wake Miss Abigail. What reason would she give?

She waited. Silence. Outside the window, a faint trace of moonlight escaped through charcoal clouds, silhouetting them against the black night sky.

Her candle flickered again. The door opened.

Chapter Five

"Becky, come on, get up. It's six o'clock!" Becky woke with a start and sat up in bed, rubbing sleepy eyes. At the door, Sam's knocking persisted.

"All right, Sam. I'm awake now. Must have overslept."

"Yes, well, you get yourself downstairs in an instant or you'll have Mr. Farnsworth after you."

"I'll be there in a minute."

She yawned widely and tried to focus her thoughts. That had been some dream and so realistic. She had felt the breeze on her skin and had seen Miss Abigail's door open. And then it had all gone black.

"Ah, well, that's dreams for you," she muttered.

If only she didn't feel as if she hadn't slept.

Still groggy, Becky reached for her dressing gown as she always did and then for her slippers, only to be caught sharp.

She was wearing them.

"Why on earth did I go to sleep in me slippers? Must be going senile."

She poured cold water from the ewer into the bowl and splashed it on her face and under her arms.

Only time for a quick wash this morning. If she wasn't down in that kitchen when Mrs. Beddows was ready to dish up their breakfast, there would be no living with her.

Becky quickly changed out of her nightgown and into her underclothes before buttoning up her dress and tying on a clean apron.

Finally, she combed her hair and pinned it up as best she could before fitting her cap over it. Next she buttoned up her boots and pulled the covers over her bed. She would have to tend to that properly later. Mrs. Beddows had been known to check, and woe betide any servant who had failed to make up their bed to her standards.

She caught sight of the clock. Twenty past six.

Panting, Becky made it to her chair at the table just as Lily brought in the bacon and eggs. She caught the stern eye of Mrs. Beddows.

"Cutting it a bit fine this morning, Becky."

"Yes, Mrs. Beddows. Sorry."

"You'll have to work that bit harder to catch up then, won't you?"

"Yes, Mrs. Beddows." Becky should have done the dining room fireplace before coming down for breakfast, and she would have to get up there straight afterward to make sure everything was ready for when Miss Abigail and his lordship came down.

"I assume his lordship will be having breakfast this morning, Mr. Farnsworth?" the cook asked.

"I have not been informed otherwise, so I think we can assume that both he and Miss Abigail will be coming down as usual."

In the warm room, Becky struggled to keep her eyes open and failed.

Mrs. Beddows' sharp voice cut into her stupor. "Becky, are we to have the pleasure of your company today or are you going to sleep your way through it?"

"I'm sorry, Mrs. Beddows. I didn't sleep very well, that's all."

"What you need is a strong cup of tea, my girl. That'll get you going."

"Yes, Mrs. Beddows." She accepted a cup from Lily, catching the maid's eye as she did so. Lily looked odd, as if she were far away and not really part of what was going on around her. Becky glanced over to Sarah. The other maid was eating her breakfast, her eyes focused on her plate.

Becky took a long swig of tea, holding her cup in both hands. She looked around the table. Cyril was pushing his chair back and wishing everyone a good day. He would be taking his lordship riding later, although the state Lord Stonefleet was in, Becky doubted he'd even make it onto the horse. Maybe Cyril would take him out in the carriage instead.

Sam saw her looking and winked, giving her his best cheeky grin. Becky smiled back. He may not understand any of it, but he was her best friend in the house right now. It seemed like years since she had felt able to have a proper chat with Sarah, even though they used to be quite close at one time—so long as Becky had remembered her place as Sarah's junior, of course.

Becky watched the way Sarah handed Lily the milk and sugar for her second cup of tea. That wasn't right. Lily was far more junior than Sarah. *She* should have been pouring out Sarah's tea and handing *her* the milk and sugar. But no one else seemed to notice.

With one last gulp, she drained her cup and stood. "I'm off to do the upstairs' fireplaces."

"You mind you do them properly, Becky. I don't want any complaints from Miss Abigail," Mr. Farnsworth said.

"Yes, Mr. Farnsworth."

Becky took her ash bucket and cleaning cloths from the scullery and made her way upstairs.

Fortunately, the dining room hadn't been used since breakfast yesterday and there hadn't been a fire, so she reckoned she should be over and done with it in a few minutes. The library and morning room would take longer, as they had been used throughout the day with a fire lit in the evening, which had been chillier of late.

In the morning room, Becky drew back the deep blue velvet curtains, letting in a pale yellow sunlight. She squinted up at the encroaching gray clouds and muttered to herself. "Looks like we're in for rain later."

She went straight to the fireplace and spread her cloth on the carpet in front of her before kneeling on it to sweep up the ash. She gave the grate a good polish with her cloth and proceeded to re-lay the fire.

When she had finished, she started on the display cabinet. From the top of it, she carefully picked up antique Chinese vases and ornaments, dusting them and ensuring she cleaned the surfaces underneath. She was meticulous about each one. Any breakages would have to be accounted for. Not that she could ever afford to replace any of them.

She'd be working until her grave before she could even hope to redeem a tiny proportion of the cost of even the smallest one.

Moving around the room, she finished up at the small writing desk under the window. One of its three slim drawers was open a few inches, and Becky made to close it before her eye was attracted to something lying inside.

Diary, she read.

She glanced behind her. The door was closed, and she would hear if someone opened it. They would think she was dusting, and the Chesterfield obscured the view across the room. Becky ensured her own body would form another block as she bent down, opened the drawer still further, and turned the slim volume ninety degrees so she could open the cover. If she was discovered, she could be thrown out with no reference—or, at best severely disciplined—but she couldn't resist the temptation. Whose diary was it?

She turned over the leather cover and read the front page.

Isabella Stonefleet. Her Diary. 1890.

Six years ago. The year of the accident. Her ladyship's diary!

No going back. That year had been so significant for her employers that it had changed everyone's lives. Surely her ladyship must have recorded some of the events.

Becky flicked the pages through January and February, conscious that time was getting on, and she was a slow reader. She still had a myriad of chores to do. The accident had taken place in August of that year so she turned the pages faster, all the while listening for the telltale rasp of the door handle.

Her eye caught something. She stopped turning pages and lifted the diary up to peer at it more closely. Her ladyship's handwriting was a little more flamboyant than Becky was used to, and her words took some deciphering. But she soon became riveted.

> *August 2. Sidney says he cannot see me today. R. summoned him yesterday and told him his work was no longer up to the required standard. Sidney said he raved and ranted like a man possessed. He is sure R. knows about us and has begged me to come away with him. I*

cannot decide. For what should we live on? I am
dependent on R. for everything, and without work,
Sidney and I would be destitute, shunned by society, and
without a roof over our heads. Dear God, what am I to
do? What if Abigail should find out?

Becky laid the diary back in the drawer. Even that little extract had taken her ten minutes to read, and Lady Stonefleet had carried on making entries. Becky could see that there were many more pages to come.

Maybe this would explain everything. Becky had to read it all but if she was found to have removed it... She shivered.

If she left it there, she could always read a little bit every day. But what if Miss Abigail moved it? Or his lordship? After all, the drawer had been partially open so maybe someone had placed it there and would be looking for it.

Torn, Becky decided to leave it behind and let fate decide. "If it's meant to be, it will be there tomorrow and I can read a bit more," she whispered before reluctantly closing the drawer and gathering her things and only just in time, as it turned out. As she left the room, she met Miss Abigail, about to enter. She had abandoned full mourning and was dressed in a light gray 'at home' dress. A perfectly respectable color, of course, but wasn't it a bit soon?

Miss Abigail barely acknowledged her and closed the door behind her. Becky shook her head and took her ash bucket downstairs.

As she descended the back staircase, she pondered on her discovery. Should she tell Sam? She certainly couldn't tell anyone else and, after all, he was the one who had told her about her ladyship's indiscretion with the foreman in the first place.

She found him decanting a bottle of port in the butler's pantry. Mr. Farnsworth was on his day off and had gone to visit some friends in Devizes.

"Here, you'll never guess what I've found."

Sam stopped pouring. "What?"

"Lady Stonefleet's diary from 1890."

Sam nearly dropped the bottle. "Eighteen ninety? But that was the year when—"

Becky nodded vigorously. "I know. It's ever so 'ard to read but I got to this entry for August second, and she says she thinks 'R.' is onto them—her and Sidney. Well, 'R.' 'as got to be his Lordship. R for Richard."

"Yes. I suppose. What else did it say?"

"I don't know yet because it took me ages to make that out and I nearly got caught. I only just got out before Miss Abigail came in. Face like thunder she 'ad, too."

"All the same. It would be interesting to find out what else she wrote," Sam whispered. "You couldn't nick it, could you? Just for one night. I read quicker than you, so I can read it all and tell you what it says. You can put it back the next day. See? They won't miss it for one day, will they?"

Becky looked at him, uncertainty mounting inside her. "If I get caught, they'll throw me out."

"Don't get caught. Go on, Becky, you know you want to."

A battle waged inside her—her conscience versus her curiosity.

Curiosity won. "All right. I'll do it tomorrow. But as it's Sunday and we've both got the afternoon off, I think we should read it together. We can go for a walk somewhere."

Sam nodded, and Becky felt a little thrill of excitement that she used to dampen the dreadful feeling of unease.

"Becky."

She hadn't heard Miss Abigail come down the stairs, and the suddenness made her jump.

Recovering herself quickly, Becky stopped dusting the large circular hall table and gave Miss Abigail what she hoped was a demure look.

"I want you to pay particular attention to the ornaments on the mantelpiece in the morning room. I noticed they haven't been dusted properly for some time."

In her excitement at finding the diary the previous day, Becky had forgotten to clean there. "Yes, Miss Abigail. I'm going in there right now and I'll make sure they're spick-and-span."

"Make sure you do. Most of the house may be shut down but we don't want standards to slip in the rest of it, do we?"

"No, Miss."

"Very well."

Miss Abigail's skirts swished as she swept past her and up the stairs. She would be going out soon. Sam had told Becky that she had ordered Cyril to get the buggy ready for eleven o'clock, half an hour from now.

She forced herself to carry on dusting and polishing.

She heard a noise. Miss Abigail was coming back down the stairs, her mauve hat perfectly complimenting her lace-trimmed dress, with her matching kid gloves and reticule completing the ensemble. Becky carried on dusting the grandfather clock, watching her out of the corner of her eye. Miss Abigail looked different somehow and, as she stood in profile, Becky suddenly realized why.

She had always been tall and slender but, in recent years, had developed fine lines around her eyes and mouth. Her lips, while never full, had become thinner and her skin had grown sallow. But, as she turned to talk to Sarah, who had followed her, Becky saw her head-on and it was a face that could have sat well on a young woman of twenty-five. Miss Abigail's pale complexion was fresh, blemish-free, and smooth. No crow's feet wrinkled the corners of her eyes, no lines creased her plump red lips. Her black hair was glossy, more luxuriant and when she moved her hands, the fingers were graceful in their youthfulness.

Becky realized she was staring and hurriedly turned back to her work before her inactivity was noticed. While she polished, her mind raced. How was all this possible? How could Miss Abigail look so young all of a sudden? Still more questions to add to the increasing collection.

Miss Abigail was leaving. Becky looked up again.

"I shall return at around four, Sarah. Kindly tell Mrs. Beddows to prepare some sandwiches and tea for me in the morning room. His lordship will not be joining me."

"Very good, Miss Abigail."

Sarah opened the door for her mistress, and Miss Abigail went out into the sunshine. Closing the door, Sarah turned back, and her eyes met Becky's.

"What are you gawping at? Don't you have work to do?"

Becky kept her voice steady. "Yes, I'm just going into the morning room."

Sarah nodded and went through the door leading down to the servants' hall. Her reprimand had almost echoed the old Sarah. Almost. But not quite. It had felt like an actress reciting her lines.

Taking a deep breath, Becky turned the handle of the morning room door and went in, closing it firmly behind her. She would dust those ornaments first. No sense in giving Miss Abigail any room for further complaint.

One after the other, she picked up the porcelain trinkets and polished them, ensuring every little detail was thoroughly clean. Some of them were so intricate and delicate that Becky was afraid they would break under the strain, and she was relieved when she was able to put the last one back.

Next, she fluffed up the cushions on the Chesterfield and the armchairs before turning her attention to the desk. Her heart pounded. Did she dare go through with it?

She hurried over and opened the second drawer where the diary should be. Carefully, she removed it, turning to the next entry.

A noise. Someone was coming. She grabbed the diary and shoved it deep into her pocket, smoothing her apron with one hand and closing the drawer with the other as the door opened.

"Becky," Sarah said, "when you've finished in here, could you come and help me with the carpet cleaner? His lordship's room needs doing."

"Yes. I'll only be a few minutes."

"His lordship's gone out for a little stroll in the garden as it's such a nice morning. So it gives us a good opportunity."

Becky nodded, wondering how his lordship managed to shuffle down the stairs, let alone go for a stroll. "Is he feeling a bit better today?"

"Not too bad. Considering."

Sarah left, and Becky hesitated for a moment to give her time to get upstairs. Becky herself needed to go to her room and deposit the diary before joining her. She couldn't risk it falling out of her pocket.

Once in her room, Becky looked about for the best place to hide it. None of the servants were allowed to lock their doors so anyone could come in at any time. Not that they were likely to, but with Lily and Sarah the way they were, Becky wasn't leaving anything to chance.

Deciding the bed was the best choice, she hurriedly stuffed it under her mattress, smoothed down the covers, and left, closing the door behind her.

She met his lordship coming out of his room. He seemed not to notice her. His stooped frame dragged along the landing, followed by Sam, who gave Becky a questioning look. She returned it with the briefest of nods. They would meet up after lunch, down by the fountain, through the little copse, and out of sight of the main house.

The water sparkled as it caught the sunlight. Becky thought this to be the loveliest part of the garden, secluded as it was by a serpentine lake. It stood opposite a Grecian-style summer house, designed by the renowned eighteenth century landscape gardener, Capability Brown. Becky loved this fairytale place, where lifelike statues of nymphs and scantily clad maidens vied with pretty lawns and colorful flower borders, tended with loving care by a small team of gardeners who lived in the village.

Today was Sunday, so they would all be at home with their families. Sam and Becky could be fairly sure of being undisturbed unless one of the other servants decided to take a walk down here.

"We're all right." Sam spread a blanket on the grass. "His lordship decided it was too hot outside so he's gone for a little lie down. He doesn't have much energy these days."

"And to think 'ow he used to be. Used to frighten me, something awful. Not so much now though."

"Yes, well, his temper's a little better these days, thank goodness. In the past, I've had to dodge many a flying boot from him when he was narked about something and it didn't take much to start him off, especially in the year before the accident. Proper ticked off, he was. All I had to do was breathe wrong, and he'd be at me. Mind you, I suppose, given what we know now, it's easy to see why."

Becky nodded and pulled the diary from her pocket. "I tell you, I feel proper wicked taking this."

"Borrowing, Becky. You're only borrowing it. You'll put it back later. Tomorrow at the latest."

She handed it to Sam, and he opened it. "Where did you get up to?"

"August second."

Sam flicked over the pages until he found the entry and read it. "I see what you mean about her ladyship's writing. Let's see what her next entry says. She misses a few days. Here it is, August tenth."

He squinted at the untidy handwriting and read it out.

> *Saw Sidney. He says R. is definitely suspicious and threatened him. He said we must go away together and it must be soon. He cannot bear to be without me and, God forgive me, neither can I. This past week has been torture. Seeing him from afar and not being able to talk to him, much less to hold and caress him. My dearest Sidney, what am I to do? What is to become of me, for I am hopelessly, madly in love with him.*

Becky's hands flew to her face. "Oh my! Whoever would 'ave thought it? Her ladyship mad for love."

Sam smiled and winked. "You never know with the toffs, do you? Her ladyship, all swan-like and demure, and underneath, the fires of passion were raging." He laughed.

Becky gave his arm a lighthearted smack. "Come on, what does she say next?"

Sam turned the page, read quickly, and his smile faded. "It's not good."

> *August twenty-first. How can I write these words?*
>
> *My poor darling Sidney is dead. They say the machine was faulty, but I know the truth of it, and twenty-five men, women, and children are dead because of it. Twenty-five dead when there was only one he wanted to kill. God forgive him for I never shall.*

Sam lowered the diary, and he and Becky exchange horrified looks. "Is she saying what I think she's saying?" Becky asked at last.

"I think so. She's blaming his lordship for the accident. She's saying he somehow sabotaged the machine and killed all those people."

"But I thought it was a fire that killed them."

"I did hear there was talk that the fire was caused by a faulty machine. Now it looks as if it may have been started to conceal the real cause. That's if this is to be believed."

"Gawd 'elp us," Becky breathed out. "I wonder if Miss Abigail knows."

"If you think about it, Miss Abigail was really close to her father until the accident and then, a few months later, she went to Louisiana to her uncle's plantation and stayed there for more than three years. Till her uncle died, in fact. When she came back, she was different. Wouldn't spend any time with her father. But also around that time, he started to go downhill."

Becky's eyes grew wider. "Do you think she told him what she suspected? Maybe she threatened him?"

"I don't know, but have you never wondered why she's not married? I mean, she must have had her chances."

"Sarah said it was because her father couldn't bear to lose her from his side. Downright selfish, I call it."

"Possibly. Or maybe her heart is so full of hate and vengeance she hasn't got room for love."

A sudden rustle in the bushes nearby stopped them. Becky turned. "What was that?"

They scrambled to their feet and peered into the thick undergrowth.

"Can't see anyone," Sam said. "Probably a bird or a cat or something. Maybe even a fox."

Becky shrugged and turned back. They sat down on the blanket again.

"Has she written anything else?" she asked.

Sam flicked over blank pages. "No. Oh, wait a minute. There is something."

> *November thirtieth. Abigail is to go to Juniper Grove. Louisiana is so far away and I will miss her dreadfully, but it is best that she goes away from this unhappy house.*
>
> *Maybe there she can find some happiness. She says she doesn't want to leave me but I cannot bear to see her with him. She is so young for her age and really should be married with babes of her own by now. R. is too cruel. He has fought me on this but I have prevailed. He knows that I know what he did, and he cannot risk exposure. As God is my witness, if it weren't for dear Abigail, I would tell the world and see him hang for it.*

Becky sighed. "That leaves no doubt then. His lordship caused the accident and we're living in the 'ouse of a murderer."

They hadn't noticed the dark clouds amassing, and a few spots of rain rapidly became a shower. Becky shoved the diary back in her pocket "Oh Gawd, we'd better get out of 'ere before we drown."

Sam hurriedly rolled up the blanket and the two of them made a dash for the house, arriving drenched to the skin. Becky had kept her hand firmly over her pocket to protect the diary.

Lily was in the servants' hall, shaking raindrops off her dress. The rest of the servants were having a well-earned nap in their rooms or else out somewhere.

"Been out, too?" Becky asked Lily as she and Sam took old towels out of one of the wall cupboards and proceeded to dry themselves.

Lily looked at them steadily. "I took out some vegetable peelings."

Becky saw the girl's dripping hair and raised her eyebrows. Once Lily had returned to the scullery, she whispered to Sam. "She 'ad to 'ave gone further than the outhouse to get as wet as that. What if she followed us? What if she 'eard? Maybe it was her in the bushes."

"I'll find out later. Work the old Jenkins charm. Never fails." He nudged her.

"Be careful, Sam. I don't trust 'er. She may look innocent but I've seen her and Sarah together. I wouldn't be surprised if our little Lily isn't behind all this stuff."

"Don't worry about me, Beck. If she's got any little secrets, I'll get them out of her. You see if I don't."

Becky gave him a weak smile but inside, her heart thumped a little too hard.

———

"Becky," Sarah said at the library door. "Mr. Farnsworth wants to see us all downstairs right away."

"What's it about?"

"I don't know, but you're to come now."

Becky smoothed her cap and tucked away the inevitable stray hair before hurrying after the maid. She was glad she had taken the chance earlier to return the diary to the morning room.

In the servants' hall, all the staff was assembled, except for Cyril, who was with Miss Abigail, and Sam. Becky had noticed him missing at breakfast too but no one seemed to know where he was.

Mr. Farnsworth's expression was grim. Lily stood next to Sarah, their non-expressions mirroring each other. Mrs. Beddows looked distressed. Nellie, the laundry maid who came from the village once a week, had a worried look on her face. Becky took up her place next to Lily and waited. She hardly dared breathe. Whatever had happened?

The butler drew himself up to his full height and began. "There has been an unfortunate occurrence during the night. It would appear that Sam, in a distressed state of mind, took his own life—"

"*No!*" Becky's scream echoed through the servants' hall. Mrs. Beddows caught her before she fell and led her over to a chair.

"Come along, dear, I know. It's an awful shock. He always seemed such a cheerful soul."

Becky stared at the butler, whose face was gray. "Tell me it's not true, Mr. Farnsworth. Tell me Sam's not dead."

His voice was unusually gentle. "I'm sorry, Becky. I found him myself this morning when he failed to appear for breakfast. Evidently he had taken a belt and hung himself. Dr. Stamford was called, but Sam was already dead. His lordship and Miss Abigail have been informed."

Becky leaned against the back of the chair. She thought about the diary and remembered the sound they had heard in the bushes. What if someone had been there? It made no sense at all to say that Sam had taken his own life. But if anyone had overheard them reading Lady Stonefleet's diary—someone who had reason to fear its contents—that would be a different matter entirely.

Lord Stonefleet! He was the one in most danger of discovery, but he was in no fit state to kill anyone.

Lily. What if Sam had tackled her as he said he would? Becky stared at her but could read nothing in her face.

Miss Abigail? No, surely not.

A shiver shot through Becky, and she hugged herself, rocking back and forth. If someone had killed Sam, they could kill again. And there would be no prizes for guessing who the victim would be this time.

Mrs. Beddows handed her a cup of tea, and Becky took it from her, wishing her hands weren't shaking so much. Everyone was sitting down. Nellie was weeping softly into an old handkerchief. Mr. Farnsworth and Mrs. Beddows were sipping their tea, and there were tears in the cook's eyes.

Only Lily and Sarah sat, apparently unmoved. Their faces wore identical expressions, their eyes lowered and their hands clasped in their laps. Didn't anyone else see how odd they were?

The kitchen doorbell rang and Lily went to answer it. She summoned Mr. Farnsworth, and he went with them. Undertakers. Poor Sam would be buried in a rough wooden coffin in a pauper's grave in unconsecrated ground. They might even use his body for doctors to practice on. Anger flooded Becky's blood. Unconsecrated ground! All because he would be judged a suicide, and he had been murdered. She was sure of it. But how could she prove it?

She felt an overpowering need to be alone. "May I go upstairs to my room, Mrs. Beddows? I don't feel very well."

"Of course, my dear. It's the shock. You go and have a lie down. Come down for your tea later if you feel up to it."

Up in her bedroom, Becky was relieved she had put the diary back first thing this morning. At least no one would catch her with it. But that wouldn't be enough to save her. An overwhelming tiredness enveloped her, so she untied her apron and unbuttoned her dress. She lay on the bed and closed her eyes, wishing she could blot out everything. The house, her fears and, most of all, Sam's death.

She drifted off into an uneasy sleep—and woke with a start.

Someone was in the room.

She turned over. Her door was closed and she was alone. She started to turn over again and stopped.

The doll was on the pillow next to her and its mouth was set in a grotesque grin.

She screamed.

She was out of bed in a second, shaking, staring at the horrible thing. She hugged herself tight, willing herself to stop trembling, while almost expecting it to start moving.

It didn't. It lay there. Inert and obscene. And it had changed again. Now the black feathers made a dress. The head was covered in a cap of white linen. There was no needle. Just the ugly grimace. Crude maybe, but she knew.

The doll was Becky.

Chapter Six

The minutes ticked by but still Becky stared at the doll. Fear twisted her stomach, and her heart pounded so hard, she thought her chest would burst. Even her breathing was labored and ragged.

It stared at her. A crude thing, made of wax, roughly fashioned into a parody of human form. Something about it raised all the hairs on Becky's arms. She tasted sweetness in her mouth. If only she had a bucket handy to vomit in.

She forced the bile back down into her protesting stomach.

Her eyes stung and she blinked, praying that when she dared to look it would be gone, and she could believe it had been an illusion of some kind. But it lay there, its eyes fixed in a contemptuous stare.

She had to get rid of it. But how?

She grabbed her dress and apron off the back of the chair, dragging them on in seconds. Whatever happened, at least she would be decently dressed.

She never took her eyes off the doll and it lay still, just as it should. How could it move? Becky sucked in her breath. Right now, she wouldn't have been surprised if the awful thing opened its distorted mouth and spoke to her.

She couldn't leave it lying there, nor could she bring herself to pick it up in her bare hands, so what would she wrap it in?

Scanning the room, her eyes alighted on her pillow. Of course! She had a spare pillowcase in the bottom drawer of the wardrobe. That would be perfect.

Keeping her eyes on the doll, Becky edged around the bed until she could reach the drawer handles. She would need both hands for this, so she would have to look away. She prayed to God the thing didn't move while her eyes were diverted.

She yanked the drawer open and fished out the pillowcase.

Deep breath. She turned back. The doll was still there.

She must do it *now*. Becky felt all the hairs on her arms rise. She was almost on top of it. All she had to do was hold the pillowcase tightly between her hands and capture the evil thing.

"I'm not afraid of you. You're just a bit of old candle."

With a lunge, she threw the pillowcase over the doll and swaddled it.

She looked down at the bundle. What would she do with it?

She disentangled her right hand, taking care that the pillowcase shouldn't unravel and drop its ghastly contents on the floor. She opened her door and lumbered down the corridor, cursing her limp and holding the pillowcase at arm's length. She prayed she didn't bump into anyone along the way. They would think she was crazy. If only Sam was still alive, she could take it to him. He'd know what to do with it, and at least there would be one other person who believed her.

As she sped down the stairs, she could feel the solid object through the thin cotton. She was hurrying down the staircase leading to the servants' hall when it happened.

She felt a flutter in her fingers.

Becky screamed. "Oh my good Gawd! The bloody thing's alive!"

"Gracious, girl, whatever's the matter?" Mrs. Beddows hurried to the foot of the stairs as Becky threw the pillowcase. Lily retrieved it. "You're shaking from head to foot, my girl. You shouldn't have got up yet. Lily, come and help me get Becky back to bed."

Her bedroom was the last place she wanted to go. "*No!* Where's that pillowcase? There's something inside it. I 'ave to get rid of it."

Mrs. Beddows stared at her for a minute. Concern was written all over her face. "Lily, what's inside that pillowcase?"

Lily held it up and shook it out. "Nothing, Mrs. Beddows."

Becky pointed an accusing finger at her. "You've nicked it. It's in your pocket."

Lily smiled at her. "You're mistaken, Becky. There's nothing in my pocket."

"Get her to turn her pockets out, Mrs. Beddows. *Please.* She's taken that awful doll. I swear it. Someone put it on my pillow to frighten me and I was going to throw it on the fire but it moved and—"

Mrs. Beddows put her ample arms around Becky, who sobbed on her shoulder. "There, there. It's the shock of Sam passing so suddenly. You'll be right as rain after a good night's sleep. Come on, let Lily put you to bed."

Becky wrenched herself out of Mrs. Beddows' grip. "No, I won't 'ave that girl anywhere near me. She ain't natural. There's something wrong with 'er. And Sarah. Oh, why can't anyone else see it? Sam was onto it. That's why 'e's dead." Her eyes wide, she pointed again at Lily. "*You* couldn't let him live, could you? He knew too much. And now you're coming after me. Oh, Mrs. Beddows, I'm that scared. You're going to find me 'anging in me room one day, I know you are."

Mrs. Beddows lips set in a firm line and when she spoke, she was firmly in control. "Lily, quick and fetch Dr. Stamford. Tell him it's urgent and go and tell Miss Abigail. Where's Sarah?"

"Gone on an errand to the village for Miss Abigail."

"Very well. Becky, let's sit you down here with a nice cup of tea. You've had a terrible shock and it's played with your mind."

Becky allowed herself to be led to an armchair by the fire. She shivered, despite the relative warmth of the room.

Mrs. Beddows took a crocheted blanket from the tall cupboard and placed it gently over her. "There, that'll comfort you. It's nice and soft. Made it myself, I did."

"Thank you." Becky felt hopeless and defeated. What was the point in fighting? No one believed her, and now that her only ally was gone, no one ever would.

Dr. Stamford stuffed his stethoscope into his medical bag. "She seems quite anemic, so she must keep taking the tonic I prescribed for her. And light duties only for a few days."

"Of course, doctor," Mr. Farnsworth said. "I will inform Miss Abigail."

"No need." The doctor smiled at Becky. "I have already seen her and explained Becky's situation. She was most accommodating and asked me to tell Becky to go up and see her if she feels up to it."

"Thank you, doctor." The cook patted Becky's arm. "Off you go and see Miss Abigail. She's in the morning room."

Reluctantly, Becky pushed the crocheted blanket aside and stood on wobbly legs. Right now, Miss Abigail was not someone she wished to see, but she couldn't disobey a direct order from the cook. "Yes, Mrs. Beddows."

Her hand went up to her hair. Damn! Her cap was in her bedroom. Oh well, she would have to go up without it. She smoothed the stray locks of hair behind her ears and started up the stairs, aware that all eyes were watching her and certain there would be much speculation after she was out of earshot.

She took a deep breath before she opened the morning room door.

Miss Abigail stood by the mantelpiece, placing a card—most likely an invitation—next to one of the candlesticks. She turned as Becky entered. Becky's eyes took in the tall, thin woman dressed in a gray silk dress. She looked even younger today. The maid dropped a slight curtsey.

"Becky." Miss Abigail's voice was softer than usual, and she had more color in her face. Her cheeks were rosy and her eyes shining. Looking as she did, she could have passed for his Lordship's granddaughter. "I hear you have become most upset by young Sam's tragic death. I'm sure we will all miss him. He was a cheerful and willing soul, and it has been a great shock and sadness to us all."

Becky stared down at her hands, which she had clasped tightly in front of her. "Yes, Miss Abigail."

Miss Abigail's voice grew harsh, threatening even. "But I was disturbed to hear that you do not appear to be getting on well with two of the other servants and have been making some unfounded accusations toward them. I really cannot have this in my household, Becky. Dissension amongst the servants is most unsettling and disruptive."

Becky bit her lip, anxious to refute these allegations and tell Miss Abigail what was really going on in her precious household. But if she said anything of the sort, she would be out of the house and on the streets within the hour. Anyway, maybe she already knew.

"I want you to promise me that you will stop this insubordinate behavior at once and make a real effort to get on with Lily and Sarah. I thought you and Sarah were good friends."

"Yes, Miss Abigail."

Becky allowed her eyes to rise sufficiently to be able to see Miss Abigail's expression. It had changed. Gone were the rosy cheeks. Her face was alabaster in its pale hardness. She was like one of the statues Becky had seen in *The Illustrated London News*. But those statues didn't have eyes like Miss Abigail's.

Hard, like black diamonds. Intense, boring into her, as if she was trying to read Becky's thoughts. She shivered.

Miss Abigail spoke. "I understand from Dr. Stamford that you are to be put on light household duties for the next few days. I suggest one week to be on the safe side. So you may dust, clean the silver, and do any mending that is necessary, but you are not to do any heavy lifting, and Lily will take charge of cleaning the fireplaces and all other strenuous duties of yours. Is that understood?"

"Yes, Miss Abigail."

"Good. Is Sarah back yet?"

"Not when I came up, Miss."

"When she does, send her up to me. And send Lily at the same time. I need to speak to them both."

"Yes, Miss Abigail."

Becky left the room, closing the door behind her, and made her way across the hall and down the stairs.

Sarah was removing her hat and coat.

"Miss Abigail wants to see you. And Lily," Becky said, and watched as the two maids ascended the stairs. Not a word passed between them, but Becky had the oddest feeling they didn't need words.

She shook her head. She had to put all this out of her mind. Miss Abigail had made it quite clear she knew all about her outburst and any repetition of that would be dealt with in short order. She wouldn't get any second chances.

Sleep was slow in coming that night. Not a breath of air stirred the curtains although Becky had opened her window wide. She pushed off the sweat- dampened covers and struggled to find a cool place on her pillow. She kept her eye on the door, certain that at any moment the handle would turn.

The slightest creak from the old house's timbers set her gasping for breath.

The minutes ticked into hours and still she lay there. At last, exhaustion overwhelmed her. Her eyelids closed, and she began to drift off.

"Becky, Becky."

She scrambled out of bed. The moon shone silver into her room, and she could make out all but the darkest corners. Not a sound. Not a movement.

Her fingers trembling, she broke one match and another. Then she struck one and lit the candle, its flame sputtering into life. She shielded it with one hand, scared it would extinguish, and made her way to the door, leaning her head against it. Straining to hear.

"Becky, Becky."

There. Again. Just like the other night. That night she had slept in her slippers. But maybe she hadn't slept at all. Maybe it had happened exactly like this.

Her trembling hand turned the handle, and she slowly opened the door.

The corridor was dark. Silent. She could hear Mrs. Beddows snoring in the room opposite.

"Becky, Becky."

The whisper ruffled the hairs on her arms and fluttered the candle's flame. It seemed to emanate from some distance away, floating to her on a breeze too slight to ruffle the curtains on the window at the end of the corridor.

Becky began to move toward it, wondering at the same time why she was doing so. Why didn't she go back to the relative safety of her room?

But something compelled her. *"Becky..."*

The dream she had that night came back to her.

She knew where she would end up. Outside Miss Abigail's room.

A few minutes later, she faced the familiar oak door. She stood, unable to move, while her mind screamed at her to get away from there.

The door opened. Miss Abigail stood in her floor-length nightgown. Her long black hair that no longer held any trace of silver hung around her shoulders like a shroud.

"We've been waiting, Becky."

Becky looked past her and saw a ghostly mist in the room behind. Swirls of blue, white, and gray shadows mingled and writhed.

Miss Abigail put out her hand, and Becky couldn't help but move toward her. In a second, she would be in the room with whatever was in there.

The candle sputtered and went out. Miss Abigail smiled, looking like a girl of twenty. Becky felt herself being drawn in, as if something was trying to wrench her soul from her body. She had to make it stop.

"No!"

She sat bolt upright in bed, the early morning sun streaming through the curtains, her hair plastered to her face. She breathed hard, her heart thumping.

Another nightmare. But so real.

She glanced at the night table. There was the candle, extinguished, but surely much lower than it had been when she snuffed it out before she went to sleep.

She pushed the covers off and saw her feet. Her slippers were on the floor where they should be.

Becky slipped her feet into them, rubbing her eyes as she did so.

Splashing cold water on her face brought her to her senses, and she peered at the clock. Six thirty.

That wasn't a problem today. Mrs. Beddows had said she could lie in until seven if need be.

"The main thing is that you get better soon," Mrs. Beddows had said. "I dread to think what will happen to you if you carry on with these wild ideas of yours."

Becky sat on the bed to roll on her woolen stockings. She lifted her left leg and gasped. "How the 'ell did my foot get so dirty?"

She lifted the other one. Its sole, too, was black, as if she had been walking around barefoot for some time.

Becky remembered. In her nightmare, she had gone off without putting on her slippers.

Downstairs, Mrs. Beddows had a job for her.

"Miss Abigail's kid gloves have developed a little hole in one of the fingers. She has asked that you repair it as she wants to wear them this afternoon. Sarah will be too busy sorting out her clothes for when she returns to Burnley."

Becky felt her spirits lift. "When is she going, Mrs. Beddows?"

"I don't know exactly. Miss Abigail didn't say when I went up to her with the menus this morning, but I gather it will be within the week."

"Will she be taking Sarah with 'er?"

"Yes, and Lily too."

Both of them gone. Becky felt like dancing around the room.

But Mrs. Beddows wasn't finished yet. "Miss Abigail will hire a couple of girls from the village to come in and help with the housework and I am to get a new kitchen maid." She sighed. "Lord knows I need one. Poor Lily's been rushed off her feet. She's such a willing worker as well. What a shame you didn't get on with her. She told me she would love to have you as a friend. I can't understand why you took against her so. I think it quite upset her."

"How come you 'ave these conversations with her, but she doesn't pass two words with me? Never 'as. I don't know how she can say she's upset when she never did nothing to make friends with me in the first place." Becky nearly said more but decided Mrs. Beddows' expression wouldn't allow it. "Where are Miss Abigail's gloves? I'll get started on them."

"No, you have some breakfast first, my girl. I've kept the porridge hot for you, and there's tea in the pot."

Becky poured a cup of tea and spooned herself some thick, creamy porridge from the saucepan on the range. It warmed her and sent a glow spreading through her body so comforting that she was sorry when she came to the last mouthful. Finished, she took her dishes to the sink and put them to soak. Lily could do them later. It was her job, after all.

The gloves were on the table by the fire in the servants' hall, and Becky opened the tall cupboard to locate her workbasket. Ever since finding the doll in there that day, she had approached its contents gingerly and today, as before, heaved a big sigh of relief when she found it full of the usual reels of cotton, pins, and darning needles.

She was starting when the morning room bell sounded.

"I'll go." She made her labored way up the stairs.

Miss Abigail was framed in the sunlight streaming through the window, as if she had a golden halo.

Becky realized her mouth was open and snapped it shut.

Miss Abigail moved away from the window, and the illusion was gone.

Today she was vibrant and beautiful. Her pale primrose dress set off her raven hair and fine, youthful complexion. The lace trim at her elbows showed off her slender forearms and long tapering fingers. She hadn't looked like this for twenty years or more, and Becky couldn't stop staring at her. To her surprise, Miss Abigail smiled.

Becky's heart yearned to look as young and beautiful as the woman before her. In the latest of many wistful thoughts, she wished that she could have youth, energy, and beauty; that she could run in the sunshine, her legs strong and her knees supple and pain-free. What she wouldn't give for a chance to be what she had never been. Miss Abigail was having a second chance at her youth, although where it had all come from was a mystery. Still, Becky wished with all her heart she could share her good fortune.

Miss Abigail interrupted her thoughts. Her voice held a warmth to which Becky was unaccustomed. "Has Mrs. Beddows asked you to mend my gloves?"

"Yes, Miss. I'm starting on them now."

"It's such a tiny hole and I do so like those gloves. I shall wear them this afternoon, so please get them to me by lunchtime."

"Yes, Miss Abigail."

"You look a little tired. Did you sleep well last night?"

"Not very, Miss. It was very hot."

"Yes, indeed. I understand his lordship passed a poor night, too. Farnsworth told me this morning." She paused, her eyes never leaving Becky, who was longing to be released from her presence. Somehow, she was sure Miss Abigail knew what she was thinking, however crazy that might sound.

"Becky, I will be leaving soon and taking Sarah and Lily with me. I doubt I shall return to this house so there will just be his lordship in residence. Given his uncertain health, there won't be any entertaining here. I am engaging a couple of girls from the village to assist with the running of the house, and I think you should consider your position very carefully."

Fear poured into Becky. "Are you giving me notice, Miss?"

Miss Abigail smiled. "Oh no, not at all. I have been speaking to Sarah and Lily, and they both suggested that you come with us to Burnley. I intend to do far more entertaining there, and I need good staff to ensure everything runs smoothly. Naturally, his lordship needs Farnsworth and Mrs. Beddows but, as I will be shutting up most of the house, including the east tower where my room is, there really won't be enough work for you. We will be moving in two weeks' time. What do you say, Becky? Will you come with us?"

Consternation had been churning inside Becky as she heard Miss Abigail's words. She was waiting for an answer, and Becky hadn't one to give her.

"Um. It's a bit of a shock, Miss, to be honest. I 'ad no idea you would ask me. I thought I'd stay on 'ere. Couldn't I, Miss? You won't need the girls from the village."

Miss Abigail laughed. A pleasant-enough, ladylike laugh if only it had progressed beyond the corners of her mouth. Her eyes glittered, and her earlier pleasantness was replaced by her usual harsh tone.

"My mind is quite made up. You cannot stay on here, and I should very much like you to accompany me to Burnley. Frankly, I can see no reason why you should want to stay. This has become a sad house for you, and it is not as if you had family in the vicinity."

Becky lowered her eyes. "No, Miss."

"Then it is settled. You shall come with us. Now go along and mend my gloves. That is all."

Becky curtsied and left the room. Downstairs, she said nothing to Mrs. Beddows. She had to get her mind sorted out first.

Her first instinct was to run away. But where would she run? She could give notice, of course, and hope Miss Abigail would supply a good reference.

But with a week's wages and no immediate prospect of a job, no roof over her head, and nowhere to go, that was hardly an option.

She sat at the table in the servants' hall and found the small hole in Miss Abigail's glove. Threading her needle, her mind raced. She needed a plan and quickly.

"Ouch!" Becky licked her pricked finger and saw the tiny spot of blood soaking into the fine glove. "Oh, no, she'll 'ave me for ruining her favorite pair. Oh Gawd, I'm really in for it now."

A sudden wave hit her. Her vision blurred and pulsated. Muted voices echoed, and she couldn't move. She should feel fear but, instead, she felt a vacuum, as if her mind was emptying itself of everything she knew. Everything that had gone before.

Lily and Sarah swam into view, their faces distorted. At one moment, they were the maids she knew, but the next, hideously deformed with great, bulging eyes; long, angular features; and skin the color of turquoise. She tried to recoil but felt herself lifted up, carried.

Miss Abigail bent over her, mouthing something she couldn't understand, smiling at her and taking her hand. Becky's mouth was clamped shut and refused to obey her. She tried to move but none of her limbs would obey her. Not even her smallest toe.

She was in Miss Abigail's room. The drapes and walls were familiar, but she could see little else through the haze that enveloped her. Claws scraped across the floor, and she felt the rush of hot breath on her neck. Then she was standing, supported by Lily and Sarah on either side.

Miss Abigail stood before her, dressed in a loose emerald-green gown tied at the waist with a golden cord. Her gaze bored into her as she mouthed some words Becky couldn't understand. They seemed to be in a foreign language. Lily and Sarah's grip lessened and disappeared. Miss Abigail beckoned to her.

She took a step forward, blinked, and shook her head.

She was back at the table in the servants' hall, staring at her finger. It didn't hurt. She stared at the glove. No trace of blood. Her needle was threaded, ready to stitch up the little hole, and she stared at it in disbelief.

"What the hell?" She threw down her sewing and stood. In the kitchen, Mrs. Beddows was beating cake mixture.

"Mrs. Beddows, what 'appened 'ere?"

The cook looked up at her, confusion on her face. "Nothing, Becky. What do you mean?"

"Didn't I... I mean, didn't you just see Lily and Sarah and me walking out of here?"

Mrs. Beddows shook her head. "Nobody's been through here. You've been in the servants' hall for the past ten minutes."

"Ten minutes?" Becky looked up at the clock. The cook was right. Yet, as far as she was concerned, what had taken place must have stretched to at least twenty. Maybe more.

Becky shook her head, aware that the cook was staring at her. "I'm sorry, Mrs. Beddows, I must 'ave fallen asleep for a minute. I'll get on now."

"That's right, Becky. You do that."

Mrs. Beddows shook her head. Becky knew she must be very careful if she didn't want to find herself carted off to some asylum.

The glove only needed a couple of stitches, and Becky admired her handiwork. Miss Abigail would have to look very hard to find that mend. She tidied away her workbasket, her mind still troubled. Maybe she really had dropped off for a few minutes and had a vivid dream.

Becky sighed. Yet another unexplained event in a whole catalogue of them.

She climbed the turret steps to Miss Abigail's room. If Sarah or Lily had been around, she would have handed Miss Abigail's gloves over to them, but as neither of them were, and Miss Abigail had asked her for them by lunchtime, she had to do it herself.

Standing outside the room, gloves in hand, she knocked and listened.

"Come in."

Becky opened the door, stepped in, and gasped.

The gloves slipped from her hands.

Chapter Seven

Miss Abigail sat at the dressing table, brushing her long, flowing black hair. Her emerald-green, loose-fitting gown was tied at the waist with a golden cord. Just like in Becky's dream.

She stood and moved closer to Becky, who hurriedly retrieved the gloves and thrust them at her.

"Thank you, Becky." Miss Abigail examined them and smiled. "You have done a good job. If I didn't know there had been a hole there, I never would have guessed."

"Thank you, Miss Abigail."

Her presence no longer required, Becky left, closing the door behind her and breathing hard. This was too much.

As if in a fog, she made her way down the winding staircase and returned to the servant's hall.

Mrs. Beddows was putting the cake in the oven.

"Oh, there you are, Becky. Mr. Farnsworth wants you to go up to his lordship's study. Lord Stonefleet requires a fire to be lit as the weather's turned a bit chilly."

"Yes, Mrs. Beddows." Still reeling from the shock of the sight of Miss Abigail in that dress, Becky made her way up the stairs and opened the door into the study. As always, the warm, comforting aromas of good cigars and old leather surrounded her. She went straight to the grate and starting laying the fire.

Hearing a noise, she looked up and saw Lord Stonefleet shuffling into the room. She struggled to her feet and curtsied. He looked more frail, bent, and doddery than ever, and surely he had lost even more hair since she last saw him.

"I'm sorry, my lord, but Mr. Farnsworth said as 'ow you wanted a fire lit."

He held onto the furniture as he moved toward his favorite leather wing chair near the fireplace. His claw-like hand made a dismissive gesture, and when he spoke, his voice was indistinct so Becky had to struggle to hear.

"It is no matter, girl. You carry on with your work, and I will rest here." He sank into the chair, sighing as if the effort of it all was too much for his worn-out body.

Becky curtsied again. "Do you want me to get you anything, my lord?" She glanced around the room. "A newspaper perhaps, or a book?"

He gave the slightest of shakes of his head. "No, I will sit here for a while. I am so very tired."

Becky nodded and turned back to her work, kneeling and placing rolled-up old newspaper and kindling carefully into position.

"What's your name, girl?"

"Becky, my lord."

"You've been with us a long time."

"Eighteen years, my lord." And he hadn't even bothered to learn her name.

"Are you happy with us, Becky?"

Becky wasn't expecting this question, but she wasn't about to tell a lie, however tongue-tied she usually felt around his lordship. Besides, in his current state, he wasn't nearly as scary as he used to be. She doubted he could swat a moth, let alone lash out at her for saying the wrong thing. "I *was* 'appy 'ere, my lord."

"Was? What has happened to change your mind?"

Becky searched for a rational explanation. She could hardly start telling Lord Stonefleet about the strange goings-on in his household. "I think it's become a sad 'ouse in recent weeks, my lord, what with her ladyship passing and Violet 'aving that blood clot burst and dying like that. And then Sam."

She heard a deep sigh from Lord Stonefleet as she began to pile coal on the fire.

"You are right, it is a sad house. And a cursed one."

Becky dropped the coal tongs. They clattered in the marble grate. "Sorry, my lord."

He didn't appear to have noticed and, as she looked at him again, she saw his eyes were focused far away from this room.

"Do you believe in Nemesis, Becky?"

That word again! "I don't know, my lord."

"Retribution, Becky. I have done some terrible things in my life, and Nemesis will exact her revenge on me, for I have profited from them."

Abandoning the fire, Becky sat back on her heels, waiting for more. There was silence for a few minutes, and it seemed as if his lordship had drifted off into another world. She stood and removed a spill from the jar while reaching into her pocket for the matchbox she always carried.

His lordship started to cough, and it developed into a choking fit that threatened to tear his feeble body apart. Becky dropped the unlit spill and hurried to pour him a glass of water from a jug on the table next to him. She handed it to him, and he took it from her, his hand trembling. He was so thin, she could see the bones through the almost transparent skin.

He gulped down the water, the choking subsiding, and started to return the glass to her. Their fingers met, and he gave a little gasp. His bloodshot eyes stared into hers, and she was taken aback by the look of naked fear she read in them.

"You're one of them," he whispered. "First two and now there are three. There must be three. She has doomed me for sure."

Without warning, he flung the glass away with surprising force and it flew across the room, shattering against the far wall.

"Get out of my sight, girl! *Now*. I cannot bear it any longer."

A horrified Becky ran from the room. How was she going to explain *this* to Mr. Farnsworth?

She limped down the stairs. The butler was nowhere to be seen but Mrs. Beddows was removing her cake from the oven.

"Oh, Mrs. Beddows. I think his lordship's lost it. I truly do."

Mrs. Beddows made a harrumphing noise while placing the two halves of a sponge cake on a wire cooling rack. "Sounds a bit like a pot calling the kettle black if you ask me."

"No, honestly, Mrs. Beddows. I was trying to light the fire, and he come over all peculiar. Started talking about Nemesis and saying he was doomed. Then he sort of went a bit mad and told me to get out of the room. I didn't even 'ave time to strike the match so 'e's sitting up there in the cold. I don't know what Mr. Farnsworth's going to say. And I didn't do nothing to provoke him. Honest I didn't."

A sudden tidal wave of emotion tore through Becky, and she burst into tears. Mrs. Beddows was still soothing her five minutes later when Mr. Farnsworth appeared.

"His lordship is most unwell. I don't know what you said to him, Becky, but I have never seen him so upset."

Becky raised her tear-streaked face from the cook's comforting shoulder. "Honest, Mr. Farnsworth. I said nothing. Nothing at all. I was telling Mrs. Beddows—"

"Yes, yes, dear, that's quite all right." Mrs. Beddows guided her to a chair and sat her down, handing her a clean handkerchief from her own pocket. "You stay here quietly. Mr. Farnsworth, would you come with me for a minute, please?"

Becky was left on her own, still sobbing.

Gradually, the tears stopped flowing, only to be replaced by a sense of dread. As she heard Mrs. Beddows and Mr. Farnsworth return, she blew her nose loudly on the cook's handkerchief.

Mr. Farnsworth cleared his throat. "Now, Becky, Mrs. Beddows has given me your account of what took place between you and his lordship—"

"I don't understand what he meant, Mr. Farnsworth. Truly I don't. I ain't never done nothing to 'arm his Lordship but it was like he was scared of me."

Mr. Farnsworth nodded at Mrs. Beddows, whose lips were clamped shut. She inclined her head.

Becky stared at them, confused. They knew something. What? But, straightaway, the butler was back to his usual efficient, brusque self.

"Very well, Becky. Try to put it out of your mind. I suggest you wash your face and go up and tidy Miss Abigail's room."

"Oh no, Mr. Farnsworth. Please don't make me go up there."

"Come along, Becky, don't be silly. Go and tidy her room. Miss Abigail has gone out for the rest of the day, and it will be an ideal opportunity for you to give the room a thorough dusting."

Becky knew there was no use protesting. She had her orders and must carry them out—however frightening they may be.

Silently, she made her way up the stairs, every step bringing her closer to the room that scared the wits out of her.

Too soon she was in front of it. She put her ear right up to it and held her breath. She listened.

Nothing.

She turned the handle and opened the door, which creaked as always. There was that smell again, but inside all seemed tidy and peaceful. She drew a cleansing breath.

Why on earth she had been told to go up and clean, she couldn't fathom. She removed her duster from her pocket and started on Miss Abigail's night table.

There were a couple of books on it. Becky picked them up, noting the names on the spine. *Great Expectations* by Charles Dickens and *Emma* by Jane Austen. The names meant nothing to Becky, and she was putting them down when one slipped from her hand and fell on the floor. A piece of paper fell out of it. Becky picked up the book and the paper separately, replaced the book on the night table, and was about to slip the piece of paper back into it when something caught her eye.

A single sheet, folded in four, with Miss Abigail's handwriting on both sides. What had caught Becky's eye was one word.

Nemesis.

She couldn't resist the temptation. Maybe now she would find out what this Nemesis was all about.

She began to read.

> *Dearest Bathsheba, my work is nearly done here. I have used the talisman and the two maids—Sarah and Lily—to do my bidding. Lily arrived as you said she*

would and had already begun preparations before I returned. She cast the spell in my room and the blood appeared. For weeks, the floor seeped with it, and she harvested what she needed. She made the poppet in the image of my father, filled it with the blood, and cursed it. It has drawn breath. Such spirit it has, as you told me it would. One day, before I arrived, it grew wild and flew around my room, shattering all in its wake.

My father is fading fast and it will take little more than a puff of wind to send him into the afterlife. May God rot his evil soul for the foulness he has wrought, for the deaths of the mill workers, and for my mother's broken heart. It is as you said, my dearest cousin. The spell has worked and I am young again. I can find happiness after the years of anguish.

Becky paused in her reading. Now the bizarre things that had been happening started to make sense. She wasn't going mad. That was a relief, of sorts.

But if what she was reading was true... If Miss Abigail really was capable of such sorcery...

Becky shuddered. What sort of house had this become? She must find out the rest of it.

Father ages more each day. He has become bent and is in constant pain. I have the satisfaction that he knows who is behind his slow death. He saw the poppet, and he knew, from that day on, his life was forfeit to me. His Nemesis. I had my failures too, as you said I would. My maid, Violet, would not succumb. The valet, Sam, was a free spirit. He learned too much and would have proved troublesome. Lily used her dark powers. Now there is just Becky—

She heard a sound behind her and held her breath. What now? Had they come for her?

She turned.

Three women, their hands linked, stared at her, their faces grim and set. Miss Abigail, Lily, and Sarah.

Becky dropped the letter and it fluttered to the floor.

Miss Abigail spoke, her voice soft. "We have tried to bring you to us. My father has done many evil things in his life, and we are here to make sure he pays. Today he will meet his Nemesis. Will you join us? Will you see evil punished?"

Outside the door, Becky heard a thin cry of anguish, like the wail of an animal in pain. Horrified, she recognized Lord Stonefleet's voice, and he was coming closer.

"No! *No.*" Becky flinched from the sound of his cries.

Lily and Sarah fidgeted, shifting their weight from one foot to another and, as Becky continued to stare, she was sure their faces began to glow a greenish gold. She blinked rapidly and the image faded, only to return seconds later as Lord Stonefleet crawled into the room on his hands and knees.

Behind him, propelling him forward and with their faces set in masks of hate, were Mr. Farnsworth and Mrs. Beddows. What were they doing here?

Speechless and rigid with fear, Becky stared at the scene in front of her, eyes hardly daring to blink.

Miss Abigail surveyed the cowering, sobbing figure of her father with an expression of contempt and disgust.

Becky looked from her to Mrs. Beddows and their eyes met.

"Now you know, Becky," she said. "It's for her ladyship. Justice for all her suffering. Come and join us, Becky."

The cook cast a contemptuous glance down at Lord Stonefleet, who was whimpering, tears coursing down his wrinkled face, his hands together in futile supplication.

"He deserves to die," Mrs. Beddows said, taking the butler's arm as they turned away and left the room.

Lord Stonefleet tried in vain to curl his twisted body into a corner of the room.

Lily and Sarah watched, licking their lips.

Miss Abigail put out a toe of her slipper and pushed him. "Your time has come, Father. It is your Nemesis."

Lily and Sarah drooled.

Lord Stonefleet saw them and turned imploring eyes on Becky. "Help me! For pity's sake, help me."

Like a dam bursting, a flood of memories swamped Becky's mind. Those lost hours and minutes when she thought she had been asleep, she had been here. In Miss Abigail's room, Lily, Sarah, and Miss Abigail had shown her his heartlessness. In her head, images swirled of fields of cotton and slaves being beaten and abused while a young Lord Stonefleet and his brother stood by and called for more.

They had shown her the fire at the mill. The accident that was no accident. The death throes of twenty-five innocent men, women, and children as they burned and suffocated in the choking flames and smoke.

And she had seen it all through the eyes of a beautiful woman with honey-toned skin and eyes the color and sparkle of jet. The woman Miss Abigail called Bathsheba. Now her identity was revealed to Becky. Bathsheba the witch—illegitimate daughter of Lord Stonefleet's brother and a black slave girl he had raped—whose hatred matched Miss Abigail's own.

Bathsheba, who had taught her knowledge of the dark arts to her willing pupil. Together they had brought all this to pass.

Bathsheba spoke to Becky, reached out to her across the thousands of miles that separated them.

"Nemesis...Nemesis..."

Finally, Becky understood, and with a sudden rush of passion and relief she had never felt before, let her soul free, feeling it soar high above her.

Lord Stonefleet sobbed. A pathetic figure of hate cowering on the floor. Becky felt her stomach heave at the sight of him.

"Please, girl, have pity. Save me."

Maybe if he had remembered her name... Miss Abigail cackled, sending a chill through the room. "Pity, Father? You talk about pity?

You have none in your evil soul and I have none for you." She pointed at Lily and Sarah. "Take him. He is yours."

He screamed as the two maids swooped down on him, and Becky had an impression of huge, scaly birds of some kind, but only for a second. She turned away, unable to watch.

She couldn't fail to hear though, as his screams assaulted her eardrums. She sank to her knees, her eyes closed tightly and her hands over her ears. She told herself she was having one of her nightmares, and she would wake soon. But she knew the truth now.

Finally, silence.

She dared to look. No trace of his lordship. As if he had never been there.

She saw Lily and Sarah in their maids' uniforms, standing calm and serene.

Miss Abigail spoke. "See how justice rejuvenates us, Becky."

She thrust her hands into her luxuriant black hair, scattering hairpins everywhere as she ran her fingers through her flowing locks. Lily and Sarah copied her, and Becky looked from one to another. Lily was youthful anyway, but Sarah was looking years younger. Her fine hair was glossy, thicker.

The three women seemed lost in rapture when Lily spoke. "Look, Becky, look in the mirror. See how young you've become. All you have wished for has come to pass."

Becky stared at her for a moment, feeling a glow welling up inside her. For the first time she could remember in years, her knees didn't pain her. She looked down at her hands. They were those of a twenty-year-old, soft and unwrinkled. She caught sight of her reflection in the dressing table mirror. A young woman with shining eyes and glossy chestnut hair smiled back at her.

She watched her reflection's hands move up to her hair and shake it free so that it tumbled about her shoulders, smelling sweet and fragrant as she tossed her head from side to side. She was young again. But this time, she was free, full of life and hope, as she had always wanted to be. As she had dreamed about all those years ago in a cockroach infested hellhole in Hoxton.

All she had to do was join them.

Suddenly, nothing else mattered. She forgot about Violet and Sam and Lord Stonefleet and started to laugh.

The three women laughed with her as they took her hands and danced around the room.

Faster and faster they whirled. Shadows that looked like the nymphs in the garden danced with them. Becky laughed as she had never laughed before. She was beautiful and carefree, glowing with life. For the first time.

Gradually the women slowed, their dance complete. The three moved away from Becky, and she gazed again at her reflection, unable to believe the pink and white complexion, the flush to her cheeks from their exertions.

"I want to run outside on the lawns and feel the sun on my face!" she cried as she started for the door.

Together at the far corner of the room, Lily and Sarah stood and waited. Miss Abigail stood a short distance from them, her hands clasped in front of her.

Becky opened the door and screamed.

A whirlwind of shadowy shapes swam before her eyes. She tried to make them out but they were too abstract. Orbs flashed before her. They could have been eyes but were indistinct and disappeared before they were fully formed. Cascades of drifting smoke swept swirling amorphous images toward her and whipped them away. All the while, she heard moans that could not have come from anything human, terrible moans of something in great pain. And that smell, of something ancient and long buried. Beneath her a chasm of black space descended into nowhere.

Fearful of falling, she clung to the doorpost with both hands. Where had the corridor gone? Where was the house? Where was she?

Eyes wide and heart thumping, she spun around and screamed at the sight that met her eyes. Next to the tall, radiant figure of Miss Abigail, two hags shuffled on their haunches and scraped long claws against the floor. Their half-closed eyes oozed with pus that ran down scaly, turquoise and yellow skin.

Thin wisps of hair straggled from their heads and wattled necks, and when they opened their mouths, they had barely a decayed tooth between them.

One spoke, its voice harsh. Grating. "Come, Becky, you're one of us now."

Hadn't Lord Stonefleet said she was one of them?

Becky looked down at herself and saw the rags on her body and bent, misshapen legs. She felt the pain of crippled joints and stared unwillingly at her claw-like hands with their long yellow nails, matched by the talons on her bony feet. A gray wisp of hair caught her eye as she shuffled forward, the effort sending her crashing to the floor as her limbs refused to support her deformed, emaciated frame.

In that instant, there was nothing else for it. Miss Abigail was waiting, and Becky had nowhere to go.

There must be three.

Slowly, she crawled to the hags, their claws outstretched to receive their newest sister.

Miss Abigail smiled.

About the Author

Following a varied career in sales, advertising and career guidance, Catherine Cavendish is now the full-time author of a number of paranormal, ghostly and Gothic horror novels and novellas.

Her novels include: *The Stones of Landane, Those Who Dwell in Mordenhyrst Hall, The After-Death of Caroline Rand, Nemesis of the Gods* trilogy: *Wrath of the Ancients, Waking the Ancients,* and *Damned by the Ancients, Dark Observation, In Darkness, Shadows Breathe, The Garden of Bewitchment. The Haunting of Henderson Close, The Devil's Serenade, The Pendle Curse* and *Saving Grace Devine.*

The Crow Witch and Other Conjurings is a collection of her previously published and brand new short stories.

Her novellas include: *The Darkest Veil, Linden Manor, Cold Revenge, Miss Abigail's Room, The Demons of Cambian Street, Dark Avenging Angel, The Devil Inside Her,* and *The Second Wife.*

She lives by the sea in Southport, England with her long-suffering husband, and a black cat called Serafina who has never forgotten that her species used to be worshipped in ancient Egypt. She sees no reason why that practice should not continue.

You can connect with Cat here:

Website: catherinecavendish.com/
Facebook: facebook.com/CatherineCavendishWriter
X (formerly Twitter): twitter.com/Cat_Cavendish
Instagram: instagram.com/catcavendish/
Tik Tok: catcavendish
Bluesky @catcavendish.bsky.social

Curious about other Crossroad Press books? Stop by our website:
http://crossroadpress.com
We offer quality writing
in digital, audio, and print formats.

Subscribe to our newsletter on the website homepage and receive a
free eBook.

www.ingramcontent.com/pod-product-compliance
Lightning Source LLC
Chambersburg PA
CBHW022043170626
46808CB00003B/1346